"Hear me out, Kara,"

Ty insisted. "You might even like this." His lips tilted in his sexy, teasing smile.

With a disbelieving huff, Kara tossed her head and prepared for combat. Nothing sweet-talking Ty Murdock proposed would ever get to her again.

"What if I said I'd make your son my heir?" he suggested.

In one deep gasp, Kara sucked in half the air in the room, choked by the sudden fear that Ty knew the secret of her child's parentage.

"I've been doing a lot of thinking," Ty continued. "Your son *should* eventually inherit this ranch. And a boy shouldn't be without a father. So marry me, Kara, and I'll adopt him."

Blood pounded in Kara's ears, and fear coiled in her belly like a rattlesnake.

Could a man adopt his own son?

Dear Reader,

What are your New Year's resolutions? I hope one is to relax and escape life's everyday stresses with our fantasy-filled books! Each month, Silhouette Romance presents six soul-stirring stories about falling in love. So even if you haven't gotten around to your other resolutions (hey, spring cleaning is still months away!), curling up with these dreamy stories should be one that's a pure pleasure to keep.

Could you imagine seducing the boss? Well, that's what the heroine of Julianna Morris's *Last Chance for Baby*, the fourth in the madly popular miniseries HAVING THE BOSS'S BABY did. And that's what starts the fun in Susan Meier's *The Boss's Urgent Proposal*—part of our AN OLDER MAN thematic series—when the boss... finally...shows up on his secretary's doorstep.

Looking for a modern-day fairy tale? Then you'll adore Lilian Darcy's *Finding Her Prince*, the third in her CINDERELLA CONSPIRACY series about three sisters finding true love by the stroke of midnight! And delight in DeAnna Talcott's I-need-a-miracle tale, *The Nanny & Her Scrooge*.

With over one hundred books in print, Marie Ferrarella is still whipping up fun, steamy romances, this time with three adorable bambinos on board in *A Triple Threat to Bachelorhood*. Meanwhile, a single mom's secret baby could lead to Texas-size trouble in Linda Goodnight's *For Her Child*..., a fireworks-filled cowboy romance!

So, a thought just occurred: Is it cheating if one of your New Year's resolutions is pure fun? Hmm...I don't think so. So kick back, relax and enjoy. You deserve it!

Happy reading!

Mary-Theresa Hussey

Mary-Theresa Hussey
Senior Editor

Please address questions and book requests to:
Silhouette Reader Service
U.S.: 3010 Walden Ave., P.O. Box 1325, Buffalo, NY 14269
Canadian: P.O. Box 609, Fort Erie, Ont. L2A 5X3

For Her Child...

LINDA GOODNIGHT

SILHOUETTE *Romance* ®

Published by Silhouette Books

America's Publisher of Contemporary Romance

To Sharon Sala, woman of wisdom and writer extraordinaire. Here's the book I promised you.

And to my daughter, Sundy, queen of the proofreaders. Love you, punkin!

SILHOUETTE BOOKS

ISBN 0-373-19569-9

FOR HER CHILD...

Visit Silhouette at www.eHarlequin.com

Printed in U.S.A.

LINDA GOODNIGHT

A romantic at heart, Linda Goodnight believes in the traditional values of family and home. Writing books enables her to share her certainty that, with faith and perseverance, love can last forever and happy endings really are possible.

A native of Oklahoma, Linda lives in the country with her husband, Gene, and Mugsy, an adorably obnoxious rat terrier. She and Gene have a blended family of six grown children. An elementary school teacher, she is also a licensed nurse. When time permits, Linda loves to read, watch football and rodeo, and indulge in chocolate. She also enjoys taking long, calorie-burning walks in the nearby woods. Readers can write to her at gnight@mbo.net.

Dear Reader,

My mother was a tiger about her children. She'd do most anything in her power to help me reach my goals or follow my dreams. She was my defender, my encourager and my cheerleader for as long as she lived. For some time now I've dreamed of writing romance novels for Silhouette Books, a goal my mother, an avid romance reader, would have championed. Though Mom's been gone since I was a college student, I find it extremely gratifying and quite fitting that the call offering a contract on this, my first book for Silhouette, came on January 31, Mom's birthday.

By a lovely twist of fate, this novel is the story of another mother determined to move heaven and earth *For Her Child*.... I loved creating feisty Kara Taylor and her gorgeous hero, Ty Murdock. Having grown up in the Southwest, I'm enamored with the Western mystique, and so it is no surprise that my first Romance novel features a ranch, a rodeo and, of course, a cowboy. Who can resist a charming, romantic cowboy with a wicked sense of humor? Not me, and certainly not my heroine. I hope you'll feel the same.

So, it is with great joy and unbounded gratitude that I offer their story for your enjoyment. May it bring you hours of reading pleasure.

Best wishes,

Linda Goodnight

Chapter One

Her father had gone and done it again.

Kara Dean Taylor strangled the wheel of her cherry-red Cavalier and splashed beneath the rusted sign proclaiming that she was indeed back home on the Tilted T Ranch.

Twice a year, every year—on the day he was married and the day his wife died—Pete Taylor got drunk and gambled away the Tilted T Ranch. Fortunately, everyone in Bootlick, Texas, knew Pete got a little crazy when he mixed drinking and poker. As soon as Pete sobered up enough to think straight, the new ''owner'' sold it back to him for a few extra bucks or a six-pack of beer.

But this time he'd lost the Tilted T to the one man Kara despised more than anyone who'd ever worn a pair of cowboy boots. Her father had lost the Tilted T to none other than Ty Murdock—and the sorry snake wouldn't give it back.

The car was still rocking when Kara slammed out

of it and strode toward the sprawling ranch house. A little of the fury subsided at the sight of her dad, standing in the open backdoor, a mile-wide smile on his face.

"Ah, Dad." She fell into his embrace breathing in the familiar tobacco scent that puffed up from his shirt pocket. "Tell me I misunderstood on the telephone. Tell me you didn't lose the ranch to Ty Murdock."

Pete jutted a stubborn jaw. "He won it fair and square."

"Ty Murdock doesn't know the meaning of fair." Even after six years, his name evoked all kinds of irrational thoughts. A vision of his laughing black eyes rose to mock her. "I can't believe you'd give up our ranch without a fight."

"Don't know what else to do. He's got the deed, signed clean and legal." Pete shifted uneasily. "Things have changed around here some, Kara Dean. You'd know that if you lived closer."

Her dad had been hurt when she'd left home only weeks after Mama's death from the long battle with cancer. He hadn't understood then, and he didn't now. She'd let him down when they'd needed each other most, and she wasn't about to let that happen again. This land was in his blood as well as hers, and Kara was determined to keep it for her son.

The thought of Lane, her five-year-old, brought a sense of foreboding. She was about to come face-to-face with the devil, and though he didn't know it, Ty Murdock had the power to destroy her.

Patting her father's back and stiffening her own, Kara headed into the house, eager for the sight of home. Leaning on the bar that divided the kitchen from the dining room, she closed her eyes and inhaled deeply, sucking in the scent of pine cleaner.

Pine? Her eyes flew open. Wait a minute. What was wrong with this picture? Where were the familiar scents of old leather and oil soap?

Cautiously she stared around the room. Gone was the familiar round table and spindle backed chairs. In their place stood a brand-new dining room set with a glossy oak finish and padded chairs.

"Dad!"

"I tried to warn you." He touched her arm.

"Where is our stuff?"

"I moved it down to the trailer."

"What are you doing living in the foreman's trailer? Don't tell me that double-dealing Murdock threw you out. I'll strangle him with my bare hands. I'll break both of his knees so he'll never ride another bull. I'll, I'll…"

"Dump hot cocoa down my lap like you did in high school?"

Kara froze. Even with her back to the door, she recognized the deep, lazy drawl that haunted her dreams. Low and sexy, with the hint of laughter beneath the surface, the sound sent involuntary shivers down her spine. She clenched both fists and her teeth before turning to face the devil himself.

Pete held up a warning hand. "Hold on now, Kara Dean. Moving to the trailer was my choice. This boy may be a tricky poker player, but he wouldn't throw an old man out in the cold."

"It isn't cold," she said, perversely. "And this *boy* is a thirty-year-old man who stole our ranch."

"Now, Kara, I'm not even twenty-nine yet. Don't go making an old man out of me," Ty teased.

She wasn't prepared for the riot of emotion that swept through every cell in her body at the sight of him. There he stood, cocky as ever, one wide shoulder holding up the doorjamb. Cute little laugh lines bracketed the full lower lip she'd always found particularly sensuous. She stared at it for a moment, fighting the memory of what he could do with that mouth.

Dang it all! Life had been good to him. The dark good looks that had turned her to mush when she was a teenager had only improved with maturity. He was lean and trim, and looked for all the world like the confident bull rider he was. And nobody alive looked better in snug old Wrangler jeans and a black Stetson than Ty Murdock.

He was cowboy beautiful, and she wanted to scratch his laughing black eyes right out of their sockets.

"So." Hissing in a steadying breath, she curled her lip. "The bad penny returns."

"I could say the same for you." His mild answer added fuel to her anger. How dare he be calm and cool when she was forest-fire hot and ready to rumble?

"*I* belong here. This is *my* home."

He smirked. The arrogant mule levered himself off the door and actually smirked, leaving no doubt that he was now sole owner of the Tilted T. With a flourish worthy of an all-round champion, he removed his hat and tossed it onto one horn of a particularly tacky set of deer antlers hanging near the backdoor. Then he sauntered over to the bar, slung one leg over a stool and sat down as if he owned the place.

Dang it all! He did own the place.

Kara backed around to the other side of the narrow bar and simmered. Ty Murdock had already stolen enough from her. He wasn't getting this ranch, too.

The tension in the room, most of it from Kara, was thicker than a prairie dust storm. "You're a thief and a cheat, Murdock."

Ty braced one powerful hand on an equally powerful thigh, his lips tilting in a wry grin. "Well, howdy, Kara. It's mighty nice to see you, too."

On some subconscious level she knew Ty hid his true emotions behind a flippant attitude, but Kara was long past caring about his feelings. He wasn't going to tease his way out of this one.

"You took advantage of my daddy."

"He did no such thing," her dad piped up from his spot at the same bar. "A full house beats a flush any day of the week."

Kara's ears buzzed and little gray spots danced before her eyes. Anyone else would have thought she was about to faint. Kara knew dang well she was about to commit a crime—murder. Trouble was, she didn't know who to kill first, her daddy or that worthless piece of cow dung, Ty Murdock.

"Dad, please, if you won't stand up to this bully, then let me do it."

Kara regretted the words as soon as they tumbled out of her rapid-fire mouth. A dark flush suffused Pete's face. She'd embarrassed him, wounded that confounded pride of his. Before she could apologize, Pete rose stiffly from the bar.

"I'm going down to the trailer. When you finish pitching a fit, come on down. Sally's making dinner."

He stalked out the door, letting it bang shut behind him. Kara blinked after him in confusion.

Who the heck was Sally?

"Want some coffee?"

Kara's head snapped around. Ty held a mug in her direction, one eyebrow arched in question.

"I haven't stocked up on Dr. Pepper—yet."

Her mouth fell open. He remembered her favorite soft drink?

Between her father's strange announcement and Ty's unwanted friendliness, she felt as off balance as a drunk standing in a rowboat during a hurricane. Ty stirred a spoon of sugar into the mug before pushing it across the bar toward her.

Glad for an excuse to do something beside stare with her mouth open, Kara sipped at the hot brew, her mind working frantically.

This wasn't the way she'd planned their meeting. He wasn't supposed to stand across from her, calmly watching her over a coffee cup emblazoned with the words Cowboy Up and Ride. He wasn't supposed to remember how she liked her coffee or what kind of pop she preferred. He was supposed to be the ogre who left her standing in the gravel driveway of the Tilted T crying her eyes out while he drove away to seek his fame and fortune on the bull-riding circuit. He was the cheating, lying womanizer who'd promised a future and then took up with rodeo trash like Shannon Sullivan no sooner than his dust had settled.

The memory of that morning was still as fresh as the taste of his coffee. She turned her mind toward it now, reliving the pain and anger, calling it back for ammunition.

They'd stood inside the open door of his battered old red pickup truck braced against a hard June wind. He'd held her while she cried, smoothing back the long blond locks that whipped around her tear-soaked face.

"I have to go, Kara," he'd said. "The gossips in this town are just waiting for me to slip up, to show the Murdock blood. This is my chance to prove them all wrong and make something of myself. I need to be more than your daddy's hired hand."

"But someday the Tilted T will be mine and we can share it. You won't be anyone's hired hand." Tears flowed over the strong, competent hands that caressed her cheeks.

"Someday." He kissed her trembling lips, his eyes suspiciously glassy. "But I'm already in my prime as a bull rider. If I'm real lucky I might get ten years in this business. You and I have the rest of our lives to be together." His callused thumbs massaged the line of her jaw. "When my rodeo career is behind me, and I have some money in my pockets, we'll turn the Tilted T into the finest ranch in east Texas."

"If you love me, you'll stay."

"Kara, I do love you." His voice was husky, thick with emotion. "That's why I have to go. Please understand."

But she hadn't understood. Heedless of her pleading, he'd stepped up into the cab of the truck, started the engine and driven out of her life. She'd given him an ultimatum—her or the rodeo. In the end, he'd chosen the rodeo, and his daddy's womanizing legacy, over her.

The agony of that memory was powerful enough to bring her to her senses. She would not be fooled by any man ever again. Especially not this man.

"This is my family's ranch and I want it back."

"Why?" His eyes narrowed as he studied her stormy expression. "If you cared about this place, why'd you move off to Oklahoma City and leave your dad to run things all by himself?''

She bit back the angry retort that simmered inside her. How dare he question her loyalty to this ranch? He didn't know all the nights she'd cried herself to sleep inside the tiny city apartment with the unfamiliar sounds of sirens and traffic roaring in her ears. He couldn't know how homesick she'd been, or how desperately she'd needed the comfort of home and family. Or how desperately she'd needed him.

''I had my reasons for moving to the city.'' She gripped the warm mug so tightly she thought it might shatter.

''Yeah. I heard you got married.'' Ty set his own cup carefully on the counter and stared down at it. ''And divorced. Pete even showed me a picture of your son.''

Though nothing in his manner said he was even the least bit suspicious, Kara's blood turned to ice water. She swallowed twice before trusting herself to speak.

''My personal life is none of your business.''

''It used to be.'' He traced the lip of his coffee cup with a long, dark finger.

''That was a long time ago, Ty.'' *Before you chose the back of a bull over the woman you claimed to love. Before you allowed the rodeo groupies to share the love you'd promised to save for me. Before I had your baby all by myself.*

She called up the image of a pale, trembling nineteen-year-old; saw her standing over the bathroom sink as the home pregnancy test revealed the truth. She remembered the smell of fried eggs the first time she'd suffered morning sickness; the taut, swollen feet, the aching back that no one offered to rub. And she recalled twenty hours of labor when no one came to reassure her or love her or to celebrate the arrival of her son. Kara Dean Taylor would never be that vulnerable again.

"You'll have to pardon me if I'm not interested in waxing nostalgic."

"What if I am?" His lips tilted upward, but his eyes remained serious, watchful. "We left a lot of unfinished business between us."

Had they not been so sad, Kara would have found Ty's unfortunate choice of words funny. Oh, they had unfinished business all right, but not the kind he might imagine. Most likely he was looking for another romp in the hay—literally—but Kara had learned her lesson in that department. The old adage about once burned, twice warned was true. In her case it was twice burned. Once by Ty and then by Josh Riddley, the man who'd been her husband only long enough to protect her son from speculation and to keep her daddy from knowing that his only child had failed him.

She'd fooled herself and Josh into believing love instead of desperation had brought them together. Josh had discovered the truth right away, just as she had discovered his propensity for alcohol-induced violence. In retrospect, facing Pete's disappointment would have been easier than living with Josh, but after what she'd suffered to protect the secret, she wouldn't hurt her daddy now.

Pete was old-fashioned. He would never have been able to hold his head up if the whole town knew his pride and joy, the perfect daughter, was an unwed mother. Josh had broken her spirit, but this sexy, handsome cowboy across the counter had done something much worse. He'd broken her heart.

Kara let the rich, sweet coffee linger on her tongue and warm her suddenly cold lips. Some women just have a knack for choosing the wrong men time and time again, and Kara Dean Taylor was one of those misguided fools. It had taken two failures to convince her, but that was enough.

Kara tossed back another shot of coffee. "Let's get one thing straight, Murdock. There is nothing unfinished between us."

For emphasis she clunked the ceramic cup onto the countertop. A bit of the dark liquid splashed out. Sliding off the bar stool, she circled the bar and headed into the kitchen. Ty stood directly between her and the paper towels. The twinkle in his eye said he had no intention of moving out of the way.

"If you had any manners, you'd either move or hand me a towel."

He smiled and crossed his arms, leaning his backside against the counter. His posture challenged her to come closer, to prove that there was nothing left between them.

Fine then. She'd show the insufferable cowboy just how completely immune to him she was.

Armed with his betrayal and six years of heartache, she marched right up to him and leaned to the left, taking care not to touch him. He shifted slightly, bringing their bodies into alignment. Suddenly she was nose to chest with the man she hated more than anyone on earth. And he smelled delicious. Her pulse kicked up a notch. Here was the warm, woodsy scent that had lingered on her skin and on her clothes and in her mind long after he was gone.

She gritted her teeth against the tide of feeling that threatened. "Give me that dang towel, Murdock."

"Give me the towel. Give me the ranch," he mocked softly, his mouth so close to her hair that she felt the heat of his breath. "Is there anything else the queen desires?"

He was strong and warm and masculine and, oh, so familiar, even after all this time. For the briefest moment she felt herself being drawn by his charm.

His hard, cowboy's hand snaked up her back, caressing as it went. Sensation as warm as butter melting on sweet corn flowed through Kara's veins. Just when she would have leaned into his chest, he tugged at her ponytail and dropped his hand. The quiet rumble of his chuckle tickled her face.

Kara jerked away, breaking contact with his body. How dare he toy with her! And why on earth had she responded like that?

Not caring if the coffee spill ever got wiped up, she marched around the counter away from him. If he thought he could charm her into forgetting what he'd done, he could think again. Once she might have folded, but now she had her son to consider.

"You haven't changed a bit, Murdock," she said in a distressfully breathless voice. "You're still the selfish little boy you always were, thinking you can charm your way in or out of anything. Well, I've got news for you this go-round, cowboy. You can saddle up and ride right on out the way you came in. Just put the deed to the Tilted T on the table as you leave."

He struck a casual pose, his face unreadable, though Kara suspected he wasn't nearly as unmoved as he pretended. "Sorry to disappoint you, honey, but this old cowboy ain't going nowhere."

"Then, I'll take you to court."

"You don't have a leg to stand on. This place was in your father's name."

"Dad intended for my son to have the Tilted T."

"Maybe. But, if you really thought he could take over someday, you would have had him living here all his life. A boy raised in the city can't run a ranch."

"I'm teaching him."

"How? By showing him reruns of *Gunsmoke?* By letting him ride the plastic pony at Wal-Mart?"

"I'll have you know Lane can ride as well as I could at his age." And every time he mounted a horse, Kara's heart broke to think of how his own father's cheating had robbed her son of the opportunity to grow up on horseback the way she had.

Ty shoved away from the counter and stalked toward her. "What about his father? Maybe he has plans for the boy."

Kara shivered inwardly at the thought, the secret raring up like a spooked stallion. "Lane has had no contact with his useless excuse for a father since the day he left. He has no say in Lane's life. Never has, never will."

Ty whistled softly. "Sounds like a bitter divorce."

"So bitter that neither Lane nor I carry his father's name. Lane is mine and mine alone." Now was as good a time as any to break this bit of news. "We're both Taylors. And Taylors have always owned this ranch. That's why I'm not leaving here until you give it back."

"Well, darlin'," he drawled, laughter returning to his eyes as he hooked both thumbs in his pockets and tilted back on his heels. "I hope you packed your toothbrush, because you've got a long stay ahead of you."

Chapter Two

Out of long habit Ty dumped the remains of his coffee into the sink and rinsed the cup, then turned it up on the counter to drain and repeated the action with Kara's cup. Ten years of living out of the back of a camper had taught him that no one else would come along to do his chores. If he made a mess, he cleaned it up. The mess he'd made a long time ago was what had brought him back to Bootlick and the Tilted T. Trouble was, he'd stepped in a bigger mess as soon as he'd hit the place.

Nobody could have been more surprised than he to hold the deed to the ranch where he'd spent his summers during high school and college. He'd come back hoping to buy a place of his own, all right, but he hadn't thought it would be the Tilted T. Ty knew Pete's predilection for gambling, but he'd fully expected to return the deed as soon as the old man sobered up. That's when Pete hit him with the truth. The ranch was sinking in a cesspool of debt, and if Ty didn't take it, the bank was going to. Ty knew how devastating such an action would be to a man with Pete's pride. Telling Ty had been hard enough. To have the whole county know he'd failed would bring the old rancher to his knees. To have his daughter know would kill him.

After three days of arguing and studying the ledgers, Ty saw Pete's reasoning. With the money he'd put aside from his winnings, Ty could settle the debts and put the ranch back on its feet, and it would belong to him lock, stock and barrel. Pete only asked three things in exchange: that he be allowed to stay on as permanent foreman, that the agreement would remain their secret and, the toughest part of all, that Ty would have to take the backlash from Kara without telling her the truth.

Kara. A vision of her furious green eyes stabbed at him. They'd loved each other once, when they were too young and foolish to make good choices, and he felt a tug of regret that they couldn't even be friends. Fact of the business, he'd felt more than friendship when she'd bumped up against him, smelling like an April morning. Kara had fanned an ember he'd thought long dead, and he'd had to fight the urge to hold her and explain.

He leaned an elbow on the counter and stared into the metal sink. Though he hated looking like a horse thief, Ty's loyalty to the man who'd taught him everything he knew about ranching and all he needed to know about being a man was too strong to turn back now. To save Pete's pride he would swallow his own and let Kara think the worst of him. He shook his head in self-mockery. She already did.

The good folk of Bootlick wouldn't be surprised

either that he hadn't returned the Tilted T like all Pete's other drinking buddies. They'd always expected the worst from him, too. He knew they'd pointed fingers and gossiped when he'd gone off on the rodeo circuit. "Just like his good-for-nothing daddy," they'd most likely said. In the back of his mind dwelled the nagging worry that they were right.

For years he'd never stayed in one place long enough to see the seasons change. What if he *couldn't* settle down? What if his daddy's rambling blood was too strong to overcome? One thing for certain, taking over the Tilted T would force him to find out the truth about himself once and for all.

With a sigh he reached for a towel to wipe the sink just as Kara's jean-clad backside came into view outside the kitchen window. Fists clenched at her sides, she stomped toward the foreman's trailer like a mad bull. The blond ponytail bobbed through the hole in the back of a hot-pink bill cap, and her white tennis shoes churned the ankle-high grass.

Ty leaned forward to watch, and a grin broke through his somber thoughts. Jiminy Christmas, that woman gave off sparks!

She bounded up the steps and stormed inside the trailer, ready to do battle in the name of family honor. Crazy woman. If only she knew the truth. But she and old Pete had tiptoed around each other's feelings as long as he could remember. Each thought the other expected perfection, and perfection was damnably hard to live up to.

He wondered what they'd do if he went over there right now, sat down at the table and made them both listen to the truth. He couldn't of course. Pete had made him promise.

* * *

"Just look at this place," Kara muttered as she eyed the old trailer house with disdain. The once maroon paint had faded to a dull violet. The skirting was pushed in at one side. The front door sagged. Even the lilacs blooming by the steps needed pruning. And to think her father had exchanged his beloved ranch house for this decrepit-looking old trailer. If she hadn't already been furious, the notion would have made her mad enough to spit nails.

Well, the trailer would have to do for both of them. Until she could figure out a way to get the ranch back from that smirking maniac, she had no choice but to stay on the premises. Who knew what madness Murdock might dream up if left to his own devices? Though she didn't want to stay anywhere near the black-eyed devil, if she left now, Lane would never own what was rightfully his. And Ty Murdock would steal another piece of her life. She and her dad would do just fine in the trailer until this thing was settled, and Murdock was gone for good. Even at that she'd have to work quickly. Though Lane was in good hands with her roommate Marietta, Kara had no intention of staying away from her son more than a few days. Bringing him to the ranch near Murdock was out of the question.

Stomping up the wooden steps, Kara yanked at the storm door. It stuck. She yanked again, viciously this time, and when the door gave without warning, she found herself backing rapidly down the steps. Somehow she managed to hang on to the door handle and pull herself back onto the porch.

With a beleaguered sigh she opened the inner door and was greeted by the yeasty scent of homemade bread. Sally, whoever she was, had just gone up a notch in Kara's estimation.

Inside the tiny, cramped trailer, Pete's familiar old recliner was settled beneath the west window, and Pete was in it. Kara couldn't help the smile that tugged at her lips. Her father looked as content as a cat in a sunny windowsill.

"Well, I see you got over your fit long enough to come eat." Pete flexed his knees, popping the footrest back into the chair. "Hope you got that out of your system. A man don't appreciate being took to task in front of another man."

That insufferable pride. Kara shook her head, the guilt of embarrassing him stronger than her need to be right.

"I'm sorry, Dad. Ty Murdock just makes me so mad."

"Always could make you madder or happier than any other human being around."

"That was a long time ago."

"Uh-huh." He scrubbed at his whiskers with one hand. "More reason for the two of you to get along now. Especially since he's the new boss around here." He held up one hand. "Now don't start in on me. I won't back down from a debt, and you know it."

"I don't understand you, Dad. How can you let a lifetime of hard work and memories go without a fight?"

"I'm not going to fuss with you about this, girl. Now, that's the end of it."

Kara clapped her lips together and fumed.

"Stop your stewing and come meet Sally."

A gentle-faced woman with salt-and-pepper hair rounded the kitchen and stepped into the living area.

A slight flush graced her plump cheeks, and the thought that she was obviously anxious about meeting Pete's daughter caused no little speculation in Kara's mind.

The two women exchanged greetings, then Kara said, "I do hope that bread is for lunch. My mouth has been watering since I opened the door."

Sally smiled her appreciation. "As a matter-of-fact, lunch is ready. Come sit."

As they settled at the table, the older couple looked at each other, their eyes holding for several seconds. Kara watched transfixed at the gentle expression on her father's face. What was going on here?

Pete chose that moment to clear his throat. "Kara, honey, there's something me and Sally want you to know."

Unease tightened Kara's chest. She watched the pair over the rim of her tea glass.

"The two of us...Sally and me...we're keeping company."

Keeping company? Did that mean what she thought it meant?

Before she could ask, Pete rose from his chair, circled the table and placed both hands on Sally's shoulders. His fingers looked worn and gnarled against the flowered print of Sally's cotton blouse.

"Sally's been living here in the trailer and cooking for me over to the ranch. What with Ty taking over and all, well..."

Realization dawned. Sally and Pete were living together.

While she and her son were struggling through life, biding time until they could come home for good, her father had fallen in love. Part of her resented Sally for taking her mother's place, and part of her was glad to see her father happy. Still, finding out that her father had a paramour was a shock. Worse yet, she couldn't imagine asking Pete to let her stay in the cramped little trailer with him and his lady friend.

Another half hour passed before lunch was over and Kara found a reasonable excuse to exit the trailer. Thanks to Ty and her father, she had a lot of thinking to do, and the only place left to do it was the horse barn.

A long breezeway separated the two sides of the barn, stalls lining each side. In bad weather the breezeway could be closed off, but today, fresh spring air swept through, stirring the smell of horse and hay. Kara drew in the scent as if it were roses. A familiar equine head poked over the third stall and whinnied in greeting.

"Taffy." Kara rubbed a hand over the velvety nose. A barrel racer, Taffy had been Kara's faithful friend throughout her high school years.

Kara lifted the latch and slid inside the stall, automatically reaching for the currycomb hanging on the wall. With slow, steady strokes she groomed the animal, letting the rhythmic motion soothe her jangled nerves just as it always had.

"You've got a lot of tangles here," she said, pulling the comb through the mare's winter mane. "And so do I."

Unfortunately, the mare's tangles were more easily remedied than Kara's. She couldn't leave until this ownership fuss was settled, but there was no place for her to stay in the meantime.

The trailer was out, leaving only the house, the barn or the back seat of her car, none of which sounded too appealing. She'd come home fully expecting her old room to be ready and waiting as usual.

To think she might never again lie in her childhood bed and watch for shooting stars in the vast Texas sky or see the early-morning mist rise over the pond filled her with homesickness. Lane deserved to know those pleasures, too.

Thinking of her son put starch in Kara's spine. Since Lane's birth she'd faced more than her share of unpleasant situations, and she would not back down from one this important.

She paused, resting her hand along the horse's warm sturdy neck. "This is my home and Lane's inheritance. No one is going to take it from us, especially a man who might jump up and run off with the rodeo— or a woman—at the drop of a hat."

If Ty thought she'd hightail it back to Oklahoma City without a fight, he didn't know her at all. If she had to beg, steal or lie to secure her baby's future, that's what she'd do. Even if it meant bunking in the same house with the enemy.

The very idea of sleeping under the same roof with Ty Murdock sent shivers running through her, shivers she didn't understand. Was she afraid of what Ty might do if he discovered Lane was his son? That had to be the reason. She didn't trust him any farther than she could spit a Volkswagen. And she dang sure wasn't about to let a man have the upper hand in her life. Not ever again.

Sucking in a cleansing breath of hay-scented air, Kara chuckled softly and hugged the old mare's neck. Ty had better get ready. He was about to have an unexpected houseguest.

"Come on, Taffy, let's have a look around and

make sure Murdock is taking good care of *my* property.''

Replacing the comb, she gripped Taffy's halter and pushed the gate open. The crunch of boots on wood chips had her spinning around before she was halfway out of the stall.

''What do you think you're doing?'' The loathsome cowboy stalked toward her.

She tossed her nose into the air. ''Going for a ride.''

''No, you're not.''

Ignoring him, Kara led the mare forward. Ty's hand shot out and grabbed her arm with such strength that she halted. She dropped her gaze to the fingers digging into her flesh.

''Get your hands off me.''

She yanked. Ty refused to budge. Instead, he closed the gap between them, forcing her backward into the stall along with the mare. Inside the narrow cubicle, Kara found herself trapped between two familiar bodies, one warm and welcoming, the other hard and unyielding.

''Well, aren't you the tough guy?'' Kara hissed sarcastically. The electricity that sparked between them made her even madder. ''Stealing from old men and pushing around women half your size. How impressive.''

Ty relaxed his grip the tiniest bit. He should have known better. Perhaps he didn't remember as much about her temper as he should have. Kara jerked her hands free, doubled up her fists and slammed them into his chest, letting go with six years of pent-up pain and rage.

''You sorry, low-down, rotten, lying, cheating, thieving…'' The invectives went on for a full minute.

She lambasted him in every way imaginable. By the time she got to his kinfolk, his intellect and his relationship to lower forms of life, it occurred to her that Ty made no attempt to stop the pummeling of his upper body. His body relaxed, he held her captive against the mare, flinching only when she came too close to his face.

"Kara," he said in a far too calm and sensible voice when she slowed for breath.

She shot a left hook to his shoulder. "And if you think you can waltz in here and keep me from riding my own horse..."

"Kara," he said again in that same close-to-laughter voice.

This time she stopped whacking him long enough to notice the quirky grin pulling at his devilishly handsome face.

"What?"

"Taffy has a cut on her left hock. I had the vet out this morning to sew her up, but she's not fit to ride just yet."

"Oh." All the steam seeped out of Kara.

Dang him. Why did he have to make sense? She'd just thrown a wall-eyed fit when he'd only been protecting the horse.

She knew she should apologize. Was trying to swallow her pride and find the words when Taffy and her bad leg decided they'd stood in one spot as long as they could. The mare shifted sideways. Kara stumbled backward at the sudden disappearance of her brace, the now unrestricted pressure of Ty's body forcing her down. He fell, too, landing atop her in a pile of fresh alfalfa hay.

Ty's black eyes blinked at her from a mere two

inches away. The heat of his breath swept across her cheek like warm sunshine as they lay in a tangle, panting their surprise into each other's face.

His hat lost in the fall, Ty's hair lay in damp disarray against his forehead. Kara's heart did a strange stutter-step. He looked the way he had in every dream that had haunted her sleep since she'd last seen him. Worse than that, he looked like the face that sat across from her every morning. He looked like his son. As if hypnotized, Kara lifted a hand to the errant thatch of hair and brushed it back. As soon as she touched him, the laughter disappeared from his face. Onyx-colored eyes searched hers.

"Kara?" he whispered, sounding as uncertain as she felt.

She knew she should move, should leap up and run out of the barn and off this ranch as fast as humanly possible. But for the life of her she couldn't budge. She lay mesmerized by the smooth dark skin, the tiny crinkles at the corners of his eyes and the laugh lines bracketing his lips.

Before the next heartbeat Ty's mouth closed over hers, and Kara felt herself drawn back into time, to a memory as achingly sweet as cotton candy. It was crazy. It was stupid. It wasn't what she wanted at all. But her body hadn't forgotten the magic that had blossomed between them all those years ago.

He was wonderfully familiar and tantalizingly different at the same time. A thousand conflicting emotions roiled within her. He felt so right, yet for her, he was so utterly, completely wrong. She'd loved him far too long, then hated him just as passionately.

The hay, the horse, the man all evoked memories of their last night together. She'd been desperate, foolishly believing if she loved him well enough, he couldn't leave her. But he had. While his baby grew inside her, he was off somewhere betraying her with another woman.

Kara snapped into focus.

What was she doing? She'd come to rid the place of Ty Murdock, not be seduced by him. Hadn't she already learned that lesson?

Though her heart thudded painfully, and her body ached in a strangely pleasant manner, Kara forced herself to remember the terrible price she'd paid because of Ty's deceit.

Ty must have sensed her sudden withdrawal, for he stilled and lay with his warm breath puffing against her neck. His heart hammered erratically against her palms. Kara pushed at his chest, wanting him gone before the temptation proved too strong.

Several beats passed before he rolled away, stretching full length beside her, one arm thrown over his eyes, chest heaving. Kara lay in the prickly hay, senses zinging, mind reeling.

Cheeks burning, Kara sat up, brushing at her straw-covered clothes. The crinkle of hay told her he, too, had sat up. She made a motion to escape.

"Kara, wait." Ty's husky voice stopped her.

Though fearful of what he might say, she waited. When his strong fingers began carefully picking grass from her hair, an involuntary shudder ran through her. Letting him touch her again was not a good idea. With a jerk she pulled away and stood, anxious to make her getaway. Taffy, relegated to a corner of the stall, turned her tawny head and nuzzled Kara's shoulder.

Ty stayed where he was, balanced on one elbow, looking up at her. "I'd apologize, but I'm not sorry."

Fiercely, she scrubbed her moist, tingling lips with the back of one hand. The feel of Ty's warm mouth wouldn't go away. "Of course not. You think everything you do is justifiable."

No doubt the conceited wretch thought a few kisses and a good roll in the hay would soften her, and she'd head back to the city and let him have the Tilted T. But he was wrong. She'd never be a fool for soft kisses and sweet lies again.

"What did you think, Ty? That you could seduce me out of fighting for my son's birthright?"

"It never even crossed my mind." His gaze lowered to the rapid rise and fall of her chest. "Especially since I never had to seduce you before."

Kara stiffened, fists clenched. The truth in his words made them all the more humiliating. "You egotistical piece of—"

Ty held up a hand in a gesture of peace and shook his head ruefully. "I'm sorry. That was uncalled for." He reached for his hat, dusting it off against his knee. "Face it, Kara, even if the ranch were yours, you can't run it from Oklahoma City."

"I was planning to move home."

"When? After the place fell apart? Have you looked around lately? Do you know how much work needs to be done here?"

She hadn't, but he didn't need to know that. "I could see to it." Kara's chin jutted stubbornly.

"Excuse me if I disagree, Miss Taylor, but you can't run a ranch on the weekends. Anyway, you never cared about this place. You sure couldn't wait to get away from it."

"I've already told you, I had my reasons."

"Yeah, right." He shoved the Stetson onto his head,

dark eyes glittering. "Josh Riddley, wasn't it? The dust had hardly settled behind me when you took up with him. So much for your promises of undying devotion. Both to me and to this ranch."

She was shocked that he knew her former husband's name. But that was good, she supposed. As long as he believed the worst of her, the secret would be safe. From the look on his face, he'd never had a single inkling that Josh was not Lane's father.

"You broke a few promises yourself, cowboy. Not that it matters now." She jabbed a finger at him. "I'll just tell you the cold, hard facts as I see them. I'm staying. In my own house, in my own room, and I'm not leaving until you give me back that deed."

Chapter Three

Ty stood in the corral, arms folded along the top edge of the fence rail, one boot propped on the bottom rung, studying the Tilted T in darkness. Tree frogs set up their mating song, competing long and loud with the katydids, and somewhere a mare whinnied for her colt. A quarter moon spilled light over the acreage so that the buildings and corrals, horses and vehicles all took on shadowy forms in the darkness. The sky above was a black velvet curtain studded with diamonds.

He glanced toward the house and saw the kitchen light come on. Kara, no doubt. His belly growled, a reminder that he hadn't eaten supper, and here it was bedtime. But after Kara stomped out of the barn, he'd felt it wise to let her cool awhile.

He hadn't meant to kiss her, but he couldn't take it back. Didn't want to as a matter-of-fact. Something had come over him when he'd felt her soft curves beneath his. Desire, he guessed. Any cowboy with a drop of testosterone would desire a woman like Kara.

But there had been something else, too. Something he couldn't quite put a name to. He wrinkled his forehead, trying to get a grip on the nameless emotion Kara stirred in him. Nostalgia. Memories. He and Kara went back a long way, regardless of the rift between them now—a rift so wide he'd need an airplane to cross it.

A door slammed and a male voice carried on the still night air. Pete's, though he couldn't make out the words.

Not until he heard the crunch of boots coming across the paddock did he realize Pete was headed his way. Illuminated only by the silvery moonlight, the old guy looked like a specter with a hitch in one leg.

"Knee acting up again?" Ty asked, the words as soft as the night air.

Pete shrugged away the question. "Ah. You know."

Yeah, he did know. Knew very well that getting kicked, stomped and thrown on a regular basis took its toll on every cowboy. Age just made it hurt more.

"Kara Dean run you out of your own house?" Pete asked, leaving no doubt that aches and pains weren't on his mind.

Ty stared out over the paddock at the big roan gelding ambling in his direction. "She's plenty mad about this."

"Told you she would be." Pete pulled a can of tobacco from his pocket, took a pinch and stuffed it behind his bottom lip.

Ty dropped his boot to the ground and turned toward his old friend. "What's happened to her, Pete? She's the same, but she's not, if you know what I mean."

"I do know what you mean. Defensive. Sometimes I think it's her mama dying so fast like that. Other times, I think it's because of you."

"Me?" The notion surprised him. "Wasn't me she married." Funny how that still disturbed him.

"Him." Pete spat.

Ty squinted through the darkness, trying to read the older man's face. "You didn't like him, then?"

"Never knew him that well, but I always sensed something wrong between them. Never thought she was happy with him."

Ty turned that over in his mind. If she wasn't happy, why'd she up and marry the man? Why'd she have his baby? The obvious answer hurt more than he wanted it to. It wasn't the first time he'd wondered if Kara had taken up with another guy and gotten pregnant soon after he'd joined the rodeo circuit.

"You think she'll stay?" Ty gazed toward the house. The kitchen light was still on, and Kara's silhouette moved past the window. His eyes strained to see her better. "To fight over the ranch, I mean?"

"Nah." Pete draped one elbow over the rail, letting the fence take the weight off his aching knee. "That girl's crazy over Lane. Won't stay more than a day or two without him."

"Why didn't she bring him this go-round?"

"Boy's in kindergarten. But Kara don't like leaving him long, even with her roommate. She'll be up and gone soon, you mark my words."

Ty rubbed a hand over the soft, equine nose poking over the fence. He slanted a glance toward his old friend who stroked the opposite side of the roan gelding. Pete's fingers, once so deft with a lariat rope, were bent and gnarled along the knuckles. White hair, once as dark as his own, glistened like snow in the moon-light. With a painful shock, Ty realized that his friend and mentor was getting old. One more reason he was eager for someone else to take over the Tilted T.

He wondered if Kara, in all her whirlwind visits, had taken the time to notice. If she had, surely she would give the old man the one thing he wanted most. Couldn't she see the old cowboy was lonely for family? Permanent family, not someone who ran in and out when the notion struck.

"You'd like her to live closer by, wouldn't you, Pete?"

"Reckon I would." The tobacco jutted the old man's lip as he spoke. "A long time ago Kara prom-ised me a grandson. Had some silly notion that she'd let me down by not being a boy. She didn't, of course. Why, I wouldn't trade a hair on her head for a house-ful of boys, but now that she has me a grandson, don't seem right to keep him in Oklahoma while I'm down here in Texas. A boy needs a man's influence, you know."

"What about Riddley? Doesn't he spend time with the boy?"

"Nah." Pete shook his head. "I don't know what happened between Josh and Kara, but I do know one thing. She's mighty bitter about it. Won't let the man near that child."

"Did you ever ask her what happened?"

"Figured if she wanted me to know, she'd tell me."

Ty stroked the smooth, warm horseflesh while his mind absorbed all Pete's revelations. He knew about young boys needing a man's influence. Pete had been that man in his own life, a surrogate father throughout his rough-and-tumble high school years. Without Pete he might have become even more like his old man than he was.

Sam Murdock had cheated on his wife for as long as anyone could remember. When Ty was thirteen, Sam went off to a rodeo in Odessa with his latest flame, and Ty hadn't seen him since. The gossips of Bootlick had predicted that Ty's good looks and natural charm would lead him down the same path. "Blood will tell," they liked to say each time Ty was within earshot.

His mother had been wise enough to know that a boy needed a real man's influence, and she'd asked Pete to put him to work on the Tilted T, where he'd learned to focus all his wild teenage energy into roping, riding and ranching.

He'd fallen in love with Pete's daughter, too, taken her innocence and left her crying. That act of disloyalty, both to Pete and to Kara, haunted him still, adding to his fear that the Murdock blood in his veins was too strong to overcome.

Yep, Ty owed old Pete a lot more than a place to live and a foreman's job. There wasn't much he wouldn't do for the grizzled old man at his side.

The seed of an idea began to form in the back of his mind.

Pete wanted Kara and his grandson to come home for good. Kara wanted the ranch for her son. And he wanted to find out if he was man enough to settle down. He could only think of one way to do it all.

"Pete, what if there was a way to give both you and Kara what you want? And maybe me, too?"

Furrows appeared in Pete's forehead. "You ain't fixing to tell her about the ranch debts, are you? We had an agreement."

"No. Nothing like that. But I am fixing to take a little gamble and see how badly Kara wants this ranch for her boy."

"What ya got in mind?"

"A little proposition that will force her to bring Lane down here to live for good."

"Ooo-wee, Kara Dean don't like being forced to do anything. You're gonna make her mad, I can already tell that."

Ty laughed lightly, suddenly looking forward to the next encounter with the sizzling Kara. "Yeah, I suppose I will."

"Then I wish you luck, boy. She's still as full of spit and vinegar as ever." Pete laughed and slapped the top rung of the iron fence. The gelding jerked back at the hollow metal sound ringing out over the paddock.

"Well, I'm heading to the house." Pete spat one last time and clapped Ty on the shoulder. "Sally's fixed a cherry cobbler and I reckon another piece before bed won't kill me. You want to come up for a bite?"

"Sounds good, but not this time, Pete. Thanks anyway."

When Pete limped off into the darkness, Ty resumed his position along the fence rail, this time staring up into the inky sky. He spotted the Big Dipper and swung his eyes along its pouring side in search of Polaris. Finding it brought back memories.

Watching stars had been a favorite pastime of his and Kara's. Among other things. His mouth tilted upward. They'd been stupid kids, wildly in love and recklessly romantic. He recalled lying on a horse blanket along the creek bank after they'd made love. A few feet away their horses nipped at the thick clover, and the sound of bullfrogs was the most romantic music he'd heard before or since. The moonlight bathed Kara's face in gold, and her green eyes glistened with tenderness as she dreamed out loud, planning their future.

"Look, there's our star." Kara pointed upward.

"Make a wish."

"You already know what I wish." She rolled toward him, her words sliding over his skin like a silk shirt. "I want us to get married and have a baby boy with your black eyes and dark skin."

He kissed her nose. "And we'll name him Lane."

"After our favorite cowboy, Lane Frost."

And she'd done it. She'd given her son the name they'd chosen together all those years ago when the stars and moon looked exactly as they did tonight. Even now the pain of that betrayal stabbed at him like a hundred pitchforks.

That she'd married so soon after he left had hurt like nothing else before or since. At the time, he'd been convinced she was angry, vulnerable, and maybe even punishing him for leaving. But when she'd had the guy's baby and had given him the very name they'd picked out together, something inside Ty had withered up and died. She'd been his, and no other man had a right to give her a baby.

As he stared upward into the Milky Way, a falling star zoomed past, glowing desperately in the white heat of its last hurrah. He watched it burn itself out, then searched the sky until he found their star. And then he made a wish.

Chapter Four

Kara snuggled deeper into the pillow and smiled, relishing the scent of fresh morning air that wafted through the half-open window. The air was cool, the bed warm and the early morning redolent with birdsong. She couldn't remember when she'd slept so well, a puzzle considering the adrenaline that had surged through her veins the previous day.

She'd expected to lie awake half the night reliving the look and feel of Ty Murdock, of the way he'd kissed her, of the way she'd responded, of how furious and delirious he could make her all at the same time. Instead, after a cup of warm cocoa, she'd fallen into her familiar old bed and slept soundly, dreaming beautiful, happy dreams that now fluttered elusively around the edges of her consciousness, just out of reach.

Yawning and stretching, Kara sat up and gazed fondly around at the room that defined the girl she once was.

An ancient poster of Luke Perry as Lane Frost from

the old movie *8 Seconds* smiled down at her, the edges brown and curling inward. Beside it a banner heralded Texas A & M, Ty's alma mater and the school she'd attended the year before Mama died. Below, a few old cassette tapes, a hodgepodge of country artists long forgotten, lay stacked on a dresser. Next to them was a small photo of Kara astride Taffy surrounded by her mother, dad and Ty at the National Youth Finals Rodeo, all clearly delighted at Kara's winning time in the barrel race. These were the memories she'd held to in those first awful, lonely days in Oklahoma City.

The childhood room wrapped around her like a security blanket. She wanted to lie within its faded pastel-blue walls and hide from the problems confronting her the moment she stepped out the door. But she couldn't. Lane's future was at stake, and that alone got her moving toward the shower.

Afterward, as she slipped into jeans and a white T-shirt emblazoned with the slogan "Every cowgirl needs a cowboy. Somebody's gotta clean the stalls," Kara reviewed her options. Reasoning with Ty and Pete had been futile. The only sensible recourse lay fifteen miles south in the town of Bootlick. Attorney James Culpepper wasn't some slick city lawyer, but he'd carefully served the legal needs of the entire region for as long as Kara could remember. At the very least, he could tell her if there was any legal way she could regain the Tilted T.

The slamming screen door was Ty's first indication that Kara was up. He stood in the back of the pickup holding the guide rope while one of the hired hands maneuvered a sign into place high above his head. He'd carried that sign behind the truck seat since his first big rodeo win, a tangible reminder that someday he'd grow roots and settle down.

At the sight of Kara storming in his direction, he called up to his helper. "We got trouble coming."

Matt Jacobs was a rangy young cowboy who'd worked off and on for the Tilted T for several years. With a wry grin, he looked down from the ladder poking up from the pickup bed.

"Man. I was hoping to be way out on the south eighty before she showed up."

Ty laughed. "Coward."

"Darn right. Little women with spit in their eyes are scarier than a pasture full of mad bulls. Just look at her."

Ty was looking all right. Fact of the business, he couldn't take his eyes off her. His belly did a couple of funny flip-flops just like it did right before he threw his leg over the back of a bull. Kara marched down the driveway, slender arms swinging, fists clenched, blond ponytail bobbing to beat Dixie. She'd seen what he was up to and was madder than a nest full of red wasps. With a curious buzz of anticipation, he secured the rope to the truck bed and prepared for round two.

Matt clambered down the ladder, keeping one eye on the advancing woman. "This is your fight, man. I'm headed to the barn. If you're still alive when she gets through with you, holler, and I'll help you finish up here."

"What if she kills me?"

"Then *she* can holler, and I'll haul your dead carcass to the dump."

Matt leaped over the side of the pickup, shot one more glance at Kara and hurried toward the barn. Ty grinned at his back, then turned toward the woman stomping down the driveway.

He let his gaze slide over her advancing form. Still a little thing, she was curvier than he remembered, her belly flat, her hips filling out the blue jeans to perfection. Reluctantly he acknowledged she was still the most desirable woman he'd ever known. Even after all this time, Kara stirred up all kinds of strange emotions inside him.

She jerked to a stop at the back of the truck and raised her furious face toward his. Two spots of color dotted her cheekbones. He stifled a crazy urge to laugh, knowing she'd kill him for sure if he did.

"What do you think you're doing?" she demanded, breath coming in soft pants that lifted her breasts up and down in a most appealing manner. He tried not to look, but Jiminy Christmas, she was sexy. Twice as sexy as he remembered.

On her T-shirt was a picture of a cowgirl in the saddle. Kara's agitated breathing moved the rider up and down, creating all sorts of wicked fantasies in Ty's mind. He tried to rein in the wayward thoughts before she noticed and clobbered him.

"That old sign had to come down, Kara." He tipped his hat back with his thumb and squinted down at her. "It wasn't even legible."

"Getting a new sign is one thing." Eyes the color of a stormy ocean shot daggers as Kara looked from Ty to the new sign hanging over the cross timbers leading onto the Tilted T. "But you are *not* changing the name of this ranch."

"Done did." Dusting his hands against his jeans, Ty squatted down near the tailgate so that they were eye-to-eye. Kara was so furious her pupils had disappeared, leaving nothing but green venom. Gosh, he loved it when she got all het up this way. Seeing her like this reminded him of how passionate she was about everything. He had the totally irrational urge to lean over the tailgate and kiss her square on that sassy mouth.

"New ownership. New name."

She slapped a hand against the truck fender. The metallic sound split the still morning. A lesser man would have jumped. Truth was, Ty would have jumped had he not seen it coming.

"What exactly was wrong with the old name?" she snapped.

"Nothing. But it's time for a change. Like I said, new owner, new name."

"Did Dad agree to this?"

"I'm the boss now, Kara. Get used to it."

She fumed as she pointed to the new sign. "The Star M. What kind of name is that?"

He glanced upward, proud of the giant silver star he'd had imprinted with a wide blue *M*. "*M* for Murdock."

"Oh, I get it." Distaste settled over her features. She clapped a hand on each hip. "This is your way of reminding the whole world that Ty Murdock is a big-time rodeo star. The all-round champion with enough fancy belt buckles to fill a horse trailer. You just couldn't wait to come back here and make sure everyone knew what a big success you'd become, could you?"

He'd sworn not to let her get to him, but the cruel words stung. He opened his mouth to tell her the truth, then thought better of it as a little of his good mood seeped away. If she wanted to think the worst of him, so be it. It wouldn't change the real meaning of the new name, and it wouldn't change the fact that he controlled the Tilted T. If Kara wanted this ranch, she was going to have to come around to his way of thinking.

He shrugged. "You know what they say. When you've got it flaunt it."

"You won't have it long if I have anything to say about it. I'm on my way into Bootlick right now to see an attorney."

"Old Culpepper?" He relaxed a little, hiding his hurt behind a lazy grin. "Shoot, Kara, he can't do you any good. Might as well save yourself the time and gasoline."

"Don't try to talk me out of it, Murdock. The only way I know to stop this insanity is through a court of law."

"Hmm. I can think of another way." Just for effect, or maybe because the fantasies in his head wouldn't go away, he lifted one finger and stroked the side of her blazing cheek. "Fact is, I was hoping to talk to you about that sometime today. Why don't we ride into Bootlick later on and have us a talk over chicken-fried steak and a piece of Berta Renick's homemade coconut pie?"

Kara no longer fumed, she sputtered…and yanked away from his offending touch. The cowgirl on her T-shirt bounced a little faster.

"Don't play coy with me, Murdock. I know all your sweet-talking tricks, and they won't work. Regardless of what you say or do, I'm going to keep that appointment with James Culpepper."

"Suit yourself. If you have to see a lawyer, he's the

one to talk to, all right, seeing as how he drew up the papers for Pete and me.''

''What?'' Her eyes went wide with surprise. ''You went to an attorney?''

''What did you think we'd do? Cut our pinkie fingers and make a blood pact? Of course we consulted a lawyer.''

Every emotion from disbelief to helplessness to fear flickered over Kara's pretty face. All of a sudden Ty felt sorry for her. His gut clenched. If he wasn't trying so hard to back her into a corner, he'd have given in to her on the spot. Instead, he gritted his teeth and jerked upright, turning away. Kara's fury he could take—even enjoy—but the sight of her vulnerability tore him apart. Not trusting himself to say another word, he clanged up the ladder, yanked the pliers from his back pocket and returned to securing the new sign. When he dared to peek over his shoulder, she was gone.

Kara slammed a hand against the backdoor, shoving it open with more force than was necessary.

''Great. Just great. What am I going to do now? If the deed is legally filed and the papers are already sent to the courthouse, nothing short of murder and mayhem can change it.'' To Kara both were tempting at the moment. Why, oh why, did she let Ty Murdock get to her this way?

The ancient wall phone over the bar jangled loudly.

''Hello,'' she barked into the receiver. Breathless and aggravated, she gripped the edge of the bar and eased one hip onto a bar stool.

''Kara, is that you?'' The familiar voice on the other end sounded puzzled.

"Marietta. Hi." She took a deep breath and tried to calm herself. No use biting her roommate's head off when it was Ty Murdock that needed hanging. She had the most pleasant vision of him dangling by his…toes from that fancy new sign of his. "What's up?"

"Bad news."

As if she hadn't had enough of that already.

Kara's hand tightened on the phone. Marietta, her partner, friend and roommate was a master of understatement.

"Is Lane all right?"

"Well…that's what I called about."

Panic shot up the back of Kara's neck like a jolt of electricity. Marietta was one of the few people on earth Kara trusted with her child.

"What's happened? Is he hurt? Sick? Talk to me, Marietta. What's wrong with my baby?" Images of hospitals and ambulances rose in her mind. Her knuckles whitened against the countertop.

"Calm down, girl. He's got the chicken pox."

"Oh, no!"

"I said chicken pox not the bubonic plague, but he can't go to school and there's no one to keep him but me. With you gone, I can't be away from the shop, so you'll have to come home."

Life was suddenly more complicated. Her son was the most important person in the world, and he needed her. But if she went back to Oklahoma City now, Lane would never own what was rightfully his.

"What am I going to do, Marietta?" Kara moaned, gripping her forehead with one hand. "If I leave now, Murdock may take a notion to divide the place into lots and turn it into a trailer park. He's already changed the name and shoved my poor daddy out into a ramshackle old trailer in the backyard.''

So what if Pete was as happy as a stallion on a breeding farm. Murdock still shouldn't have run him out of his own house.

"If it's really that bad, you'd better hang around until things are settled. The only thing to do is take Lane down there with you."

Kara's heart fell all the way to her ankles. "I can't bring him here now," she shrieked. She didn't even want him in the same state with Ty Murdock.

"Then come home and forget about that ranch. I don't know what I'd do without you, anyway. Ever since you came in as my partner and business manager, the Western-wear shop has grown like crazy."

Kara pictured her redheaded friend pacing restlessly back and forth as she stated her case. Never one to keep still, Marietta was most likely folding clothes, planning a new layout for the summer catalog and making dinner, all while she made perfectly good sense of Kara's life.

"You've made a decent life here, Kara. Why give it up when the risks are so great? Tell that mangy cowpoke he can have the ranch. Come back to Oklahoma City where you and Lane will never have to run into him again."

"No. This ranch is Lane's birthright. What kind of mother would I be if I let him lose it?"

Marietta let out an exasperated sigh. "You can't have it both ways. If you regain the ranch, Lane will eventually have to live there, anyway. That's the whole idea, isn't it? So, if that's what you really want, go for it, girl. A showdown is coming sooner or later, so why not just get it over with?"

A tingle of fear skittered through Kara's chest. It was what she wanted, what she'd always dreamed of, but... "What if someone finds out?"

"From what you've told me, Lane looks nothing at all like his father."

"Except for the eyes."

And the nose and the mouth. And the way he tilts his head right before he laughs. Details she'd never processed until Ty came ambling back into her life.

"Then no one will be the wiser. Lane's own grand-dad hasn't noticed, so why would we expect Murdock to be any different. With these chicken pox all over Lane's sweet little face, *you* won't even recognize him."

Kara's focus drifted around the familiar kitchen while the phone line hummed in her ear. Even with Ty's scant furnishings filling the interior now instead of her family's, the ranch house was home like no other place would ever be. It gave her the sense of belonging, of security that she wanted for her son. Every child deserved strong roots.

Could she keep her father and Ty from finding out the truth about Lane while she fought to regain the ranch? The idea scared her more than she wanted to admit, but what else could she do?

Marietta made it all sound so easy, and maybe she was right. No one even suspected that Lane belonged to anyone other than Kara's former husband. People usually saw what they expected to see, and they expected to see Josh Riddley's son, not Ty Murdock's. As long as she could keep up the charade, no one need ever know.

"Kara," Marietta's voice interrupted her thoughts, "there's something else I'd better tell you."

"I've had all the surprises I can take, so just say it. Please."

"Josh came in the store today making his usual threats."

Fear gripped her heart with icy fingers. "What did he say?"

"Same old stuff. Rodeo is a real small world. Sooner or later he'll catch you alone and you'll wish you'd treated him better. That kind of garbage."

"He still wants to punish me for leaving."

Though they hadn't lived together for nearly three years, her bullying ex-husband came around often enough to keep her on edge. A rodeo bum, he traveled the circuits winning enough to keep going, but never enough to make the finals. Losing was his favorite excuse to get drunk. He didn't want her or Lane, but had some perverse need to make them suffer. Only by signing an agreement never to ask for child support had she managed to get him to give up all rights to Lane.

Having Josh Riddley back in Oklahoma City was worse than having her son in the same town with Ty.

She took a long, shuddering breath and said, "Start packing Lane's things. I'm on my way."

Ty wiped his sleeve across the dust Kara's red Cavalier spewed into his face as she veered around his truck and barreled past him and the new Star M sign. Kara never even glanced his way.

"Wonder where she's going in such an all-fired hurry?" Matt had returned to his perch on the ladder.

Heart sinking, Ty stared after the rapidly disappearing compact. "Probably heading on back to Okie City."

"Didn't stick around long, did she?"

Disappointment seeped into Ty as he bent to gather the tools tossed helter-skelter around the truck bed. He'd blown it. If Kara was gone for good, he'd blown the only chance he'd have to cancel all his old debts and break the curse of Sam Murdock.

Mindlessly he kicked a roll of barbed wire.

Chapter Five

By the time Kara drove to Oklahoma City and back, her neck ached and a dull pain throbbed above her right eye. Darkness had come to the Tilted T. She corrected herself, bitterly reminded that it was no longer the Tilted T but the Star M, compliments of the egotistical Murdock.

"Not for long," she muttered as she pulled into the wonderfully familiar drive alongside the house.

Lane lay in the back seat mercifully asleep, thanks to a combination of Benadryl and Tylenol prescribed by his pediatrician. Kara glanced over the seat and sighed tiredly. Poor little man, his whole body looked like a mushroom pizza. He was in for a miserable few days.

Without bothering to lock the car, she carried the sleeping child across the dewy grass toward the ranch house. Though the yard was dark, she crossed it by memory, relishing the familiarity. Crickets chirped and a rabbit bolted from his hiding spot in the weed-choked flower bed.

As she reached the back step, to her surprise, the porch light came on. Her head jerked up at the sight.

Ty appeared in the open doorway, the sculpted angles of his face illuminated by the yellow bug bulb. For some silly reason she couldn't fathom, he looked relieved. When he spoke, his voice was soft and welcoming as though it was the most natural thing in the world for her to come carrying their child in from the car. Something deep inside her seized upward.

"What have you got there?"

Instantly, the purl of response withered as every protective instinct went on full alert. She hadn't expected Murdock to be standing within inches of her baby—his baby—and fear rose up inside her like a twenty-four-hour virus. She hitched the limp child a little closer to her chest and murmured, "A sick boy."

He pushed the screen open and reached out. "Here, he looks heavy. Let me take him."

"No," she almost shouted, jerking back so hard, the boy stirred and mumbled in his sleep. At Ty's bewildered look, she steadied herself, quelling her jumpy nerves. "Uh, I mean, he might be scared if he wakes up to a stranger's face."

"Oh, sure." Ty dropped his hands and backed away, turning toward the hall. "Which room do you want him in?"

She breathed a momentary sigh of relief. The sooner she had Lane safely tucked in bed, the better, though she had no idea how she'd keep her son away from Ty in the days to come.

"Mine, of course. I can take better care of him that way."

Kara followed Ty down the hall, an action she soon regretted because her traitorous mind jumped from worrying about her child to admiring the lean cowboy body ambling along in front of her. He was dressed in a black T-shirt that showed the perfect vee of his shoulders and waist, a tantalizing sight even if she did hate his guts—and she most certainly did. The fresh soap scent of his recent shower teased her nose. Dang him, why did he always have to smell so good? He should smell as rotten as his black heart.

Like the perfect host, he pushed open the door of her bedroom, crossed the floor and turned back the covers of her bed. If she hadn't been so tired, she'd have hated him a little more for playing host in her house. Instead, Kara eased the pajama-clad child onto the mattress and pulled up the sheet.

"What's wrong with him?" Ty stared down at the child, his voice quiet.

"Chicken pox."

Ty stiffened and backed away. "Chicken pox?"

"Yes." She took note of his wariness. The man had gone absolutely pale. "Is that a problem?"

"Uh, no." He eased to the doorway and gripped the knob, his dark eyes glued to the sleeping child. "No problem."

"Then why are you acting so weird?"

"I don't know if I've ever had the chicken pox."

"You don't know?" She clapped a hand to her mouth, unsuccessfully stifling a laugh.

At the sound, the child stirred, whimpering in his sleep. Both adults cast cautious glances toward the bed and eased out of the room. Still grinning, Kara left the light on in case he awoke in her absence.

"Oh, this is rich," she said when they reached the living room. "The all-round cowboy with spots."

Nothing would please her more than giving Ty Murdock a good dose of festering sores.

He didn't look too thrilled at the notion. "Don't kids take shots for that stuff these days?"

"The doctor says they're not 100 percent effective. He'd seen several cases in the past few weeks." Rubbing at her aching neck, Kara flipped on the kitchen light, more than a little gleeful at his discomfort. It kept her from thinking about how good Ty smelled. "I'm having some cocoa. Want some?"

She could have bitten her own tongue off for asking such a thing. Why she'd done it, she didn't know. Perhaps because the house was so cozy and familiar, and standing in the kitchen needling Ty carried her back to much happier times.

Ty nodded absently. "Maybe I should call my mom in the morning just to be certain."

He was still fretting about the chicken pox. With one hand on the cabinet door Kara glanced over her shoulder at Ty's worried expression and giggled. The sound brought a sheepish grin to Ty's lips. He shrugged and gave up the subject, reaching above her for the mugs.

Kara turned to avoid contact but, too late, she was trapped against the counter by Ty's strong, hard physique. His hip bumped her belly, and a long-dormant need stirred to life inside her. The only escape was to jump in the kitchen sink, so she held her ground, her flesh tingling everywhere he touched. Why didn't he just go away?

"I thought you were gone for good." Ty's chest vibrated with the murmured words.

"You wish."

He paused. "Actually, I don't."

That was the last thing she'd expected to hear. And also the last thing she wanted to hear, considering the heat of his chest muscles hovering somewhere near her averted cheek. She could scarcely breathe. Why didn't he move?

"Don't be nice, Murdock. Nothing you can say or do will change the way I feel about you." She was trying for flippant, but her voice betrayed the battle waging within and came out more like a plea.

"I could say the same."

What did he mean? That he hated her, too? Her head jerked up. His eyes were ablaze with emotion, all right, but it didn't look a thing like hatred.

She swallowed, her pulse fluttering like a flock of startled blackbirds. She despised this man. Why couldn't he get that through his thick head? And why didn't he back off just a little? The scent of his shower, the masculine heat of him stirred up things better left alone. She swallowed hard.

One arm on either side of her, Ty set the mugs on the counter at her back and leaned forward. All the while her mind screamed, "Don't touch me," but her body couldn't move. When Ty's hands skimmed up her arms, she shuddered, cursing her own weakness. How could she stand here and let him touch her—want him to touch her—after all the suffering he'd caused?

"Kara," he said softly, his black eyes burning holes in her resistance as two strong hands slid around to massage the knot in her shoulder. "Here?"

"Mmm." He'd gone right to the spot that was killing her. Well, the only spot she'd let him rub, anyway.

She should tell him to go suck an egg, but his powerful bull-rider hands felt so good, and it had been a very long time since anyone had rubbed anything of hers that ached.

Josh had only been interested in his own aches, his own desires, not hers. Funny how this man who'd never been her husband instinctively responded to her unspoken needs, touching her in a far different way than Josh ever had.

She closed her eyes and let her head go limp, giving in to the delicious sensation of warm, kneading fingers. The old house settled around them, quiet except for the hum of the refrigerator and the occasional click of the digital clock on the cook stove. Everything was so wonderfully familiar, from the kitchen to the man.

But Kara couldn't ignore the much more disturbing sensations. The lower half of Ty's body leaned against hers, his chest so near that she could hear the erratic thudding of his heart and feel the firm musculature that made him strong enough to stay on a writhing, two-thousand-pound animal. His warm breath ruffled her hair so that she knew he was looking down, watching her.

Tension sprang up within her that had nothing to do with the ache in her shoulder and everything to do with Ty Murdock. She'd been lonely for so very long that for a moment Kara wondered what it would be like to forgive and forget and go with the feelings resurfacing between them.

But before she could make such a foolish move, a frightened cry ripped through the house, slapping some sense into her. "Mommy! Mommy!"

Her child was the impetus Kara needed. Shaking like a leaf in a tornado, she shoved around Ty and flew down the hall to the most important reason why she would never forgive and forget.

Ty stood in the doorway watching Kara cradle her feverish, itching son against her chest. She went through all the motherly gestures, one hand feeling his forehead as she rocked and murmured to the boy. She smoothed his thick blond hair back from a sweaty brow. She placed a soft kiss against his temple.

An odd sensation rose and fluttered in Ty's belly, a feeling he had no name for. The desire he'd experienced in the kitchen he understood. Wanting an attractive woman like Kara was a given, and he sure hadn't forgotten how good it could be between them. But this strange longing, the sudden awareness of how right Kara and the little boy looked in this house pounded at him like the hooves of a Brahma bull.

Guilt. That had to be it. This ranch belonged to them much more than it did to him.

Dang Pete for putting him in this situation.

"I'm hot, Mommy." The little blond boy with his mother's heart-shaped face whimpered.

"I know, sweetie," Kara crooned, glancing at her watch. "Mommy will get your medicine and a cool cloth to wash you off. That should help."

She eased him back against the pillows and brushed his hair away from his face. "Are you hungry?"

Lane's throat bobbed. He ran his tongue over cracked lips. "Thirsty."

"Okay. What would you like? Some juice?"

Ty pushed away from the doorjamb and took one step into the room. "There's milk and juice in the fridge."

Kara's head swiveled toward him, surprise on her

face, apparently unaware that he'd followed. A faint blush tinged her cheekbones but she met his steady, probing gaze.

"Pop, Mommy," the child whimpered, drawing the attention back to himself. His glazed eyes flickered to Ty, then returned to his mother.

"Sorry," Ty lifted his palms upward. "I'm all out of soda pop." He really was sorry about that.

"I brought some pop and other things with me, but they're still out in the car." Kara patted her son's cheek and started to rise from the bed.

Ty caught her line of thought and held out a hand to stop her. "Take care of Lane. I'll get your things."

Ty quickly covered the distance from house to car, the vision of Kara and her child sharply imprinted on his mind. She was a good mother, as he knew she would be. He'd been prepared for that. But he hadn't been prepared for the way he felt to see her caring for her child. He'd known he still had feelings for her; that was partly why he'd agreed to this crazy deal with Pete, but he hadn't known what it would do to him to watch her soothe and comfort her fussy child—the child that should have been his. Nor had he known how desperately he wanted her, even with another man's child in her arms. He resented the heck out of what she'd done, but his body still wanted her.

Reaching the car, he opened the door and leaned in, bumping his head against the low frame.

"Damn little cars." Give him an oversize pickup truck any day of the week.

Rubbing at the spot, he froze in place. The scent of Kara's perfume still lingered in the dimly lit confines of her car. Knees suddenly weak, Ty slumped down into the passenger's seat. His head dropped back against the headrest.

"Ah, Kara. Kara." What was she doing to him? Two days of her feisty company, her sweet feminine fragrance filling the house, and he was behaving like a hormonal teenager.

His eyes traveled over the dark back seat where a beleaguered stuffed animal stared up at him with one eye. The boy. He hadn't expected the rush of tenderness, the surge of protectiveness the boy had roused in him. Poor little critter, abandoned by his own father. Ty knew how bad that hurt, and Kara's boy, Pete's grandchild, deserved better.

Ty reached for the grocery bag resting on the back seat. An overnight bag speckled with cartoon characters lay beside it. He stashed it under his arm and hefted the groceries, then scooped the flop-eared blue dog into the other hand. Slamming the door with his hip, he started across the dimly lit yard.

If he gave Kara the ranch, she'd kick his butt out and cheerfully run over him with this silly little car. A dead cowboy can't make amends or keep promises. But if he didn't give her what she wanted, she just might go back to Oklahoma and never return. And that wouldn't do. It wouldn't do at all.

Now that he'd seen her devotion to Lane, he knew what it would take to keep her here. Knowing Kara Dean, he'd have to force her hand, but if he played his cards right, they could all have what they wanted. He smiled a little, thinking of the impending confrontation. The way he saw it, life was a gamble—and he was a dang good poker player with an ace up his sleeve.

He kicked at the backdoor, caught the old screen on

his boot as it bounced open, scuttled through and let it clap shut against his backside.

Inside the kitchen he unloaded the paper sack, noting that most of the items were specifically for the sick boy. Not that he was surprised. As he opened the soda and poured the fizzing contents into a glass, the two unused coffee mugs caught his attention. They still sat on the counter exactly where he'd put them before Kara had stolen his senses. He filled the cups with water and stuck them in the microwave, then reached in the cabinet for hot chocolate mix. They'd probably be up for a while.

Chapter Six

With a weary sigh Kara rotated her aching neck from one side to the other and headed down the hall toward the bathroom. Aspirin. She needed aspirin.

"Lane asleep?"

Kara blinked in surprise, her pulse doing a little jitterbug. Ty stood in shadow at the opposite end of the hall, holding a cup in each hand. The smell of warm chocolate filled the space between them.

"I thought you went to bed."

"Nah." He motioned with his chin. "Come sit down and drink some cocoa. You look beat."

The notion of sipping hot chocolate in the middle of the night with Ty Murdock both appealed and repelled, but she was just too danged weary to deal with the conflict.

"Let me get some aspirin first."

Ty looked down at the pocket of his T-shirt. "Got some right here. Come on."

Without waiting for a reply, he turned and led the

way through the living room toward the front door. For the life of her, Kara didn't know why she followed. Doing so was certainly not a sound idea, but after he'd anticipated her need of aspirin, she was curious. What was he up to?

The old storm door creaked open and the lamp from the living room cast a butter-yellow rectangle across the porch, eliminating the need for further light. Ty settled on the top step, making room for Kara to join him. After a long moment's hesitation in which she mentally measured the inches between their bodies, she capitulated. From this spot near the window, she could easily hear Lane if he called for her.

Drawing her legs up under her chin, she took the extended cup of chocolate, balanced it on her knees and sipped gratefully.

"Thank you. This is just what I needed."

"Do you realize that's the first nice thing you've said to me since you got here?"

She heard the smile in his words. "Would you rather I scream and throw the hot chocolate at you?"

"Wouldn't be the first time."

She allowed herself a tired giggle. "Where are those aspirin you promised?"

His calloused hand nudged hers, lingering just long enough to draw her gaze upward. What she saw there puzzled her, creating anxiety…and something more disturbing. Ty searched her face, asking some silent question that she had no wish to answer. She drew away, breaking contact with his warm skin, then downed the pills with a sip of cocoa.

The warm air pulsed with the song of tree frogs. Ty shifted sideways, propped one boot on the top step and stretched the other out on the grass below. "Remember how we used to sit out on nights like this and talk? If there was one thing we did well, it was talk.''

''Yeah.'' The other thing they were good at vibrated in the silence. ''I remember.'' She had to stop this reminiscent nonsense before it got started. ''But it's true what they say, Ty. You can't go back.''

Rotating the mug between his palms, Ty asked, ''Wonder why that is?''

Kara didn't answer. How could she explain that some things hurt too much to ever chance them happening again? Going back only meant another opportunity to make unbearable mistakes.

Ty aimed his cup into the darkness. ''Lightning bugs are out.''

''So they are.'' Relaxing a little, Kara put her feet down on the top step to watch the tiny fireflies perform their mating dance. To ease her aching neck, Kara pulled the scrunchie from her ponytail and bent forward, rubbing her tense muscles. The motion triggered the memory of Ty's massage in the kitchen, of how good it had felt, of how good he had felt.

Abruptly she tossed her head back and dropped her hands. Her hair tumbled around her shoulders, drawing Ty's gaze.

He thought she looked incredibly sexy, sitting there with her hair wild and her eyelids droopy with sleep. She still wore the cowgirl shirt that had sent his fantasies into orbit that morning, though now the rider rose and fell in a slow rhythm upon Kara's breast. The motion was even more erotic. He tried washing the thought away with a gulp of cocoa, but it persisted.

They talked of mundane things, of Kara's shop, of Ty's participation in the National Finals and Pete's bad knee.

"How's your mama?" Kara asked, the pull of memories as sweet as the taste of chocolate.

"Good." The little lines around Ty's eyes crinkled. "Still fixing all the bleached-blond hairdos in Bootlick."

"Holly still selling cars in Dallas?"

"Owns the dealership now. That's where I got my pickup."

"Bet she didn't even give you a discount." Kara spoke with affection, remembering the dark-haired younger sister who'd been determined to make something of her life.

Ty laughed. "She knocked off a couple thousand after I baby-sat her girls while she and Darrin went to Vegas."

Ty Murdock baby-sitting. Kara couldn't imagine. Of course, she'd never imagined sitting on the front porch carrying on a civil conversation with him, either. Setting the cocoa on the cool concrete, she unlaced her tennis shoes and removed them, stretching her legs out.

"Daddy said Jolene got married again."

Ty poked at the grass with his boot toe. Sadness tinged his words. "Three lousy husbands, and she's still marrying guys who treat her like dirt. She's pregnant again, too."

Kara shook her head, equally sad that Ty's pretty older sister had made such terrible choices. "Funny how some women seem to make the same mistakes over and over." She rubbed her citified feet over the damp ticklish grass, murmuring almost to herself. "I'll never be that stupid again."

"You don't believe in second chances?"

"Nope." She didn't dare say that Josh *had* been her

second chance. Two broken relationships, two times when she'd foolishly believed a man's promises was enough for her to know she couldn't trust her own judgment in matters of the heart. Kara pulled her feet back onto the cement step. Bits of grass clung to her toes. "I have a son to raise. He's my life. I don't need or want anyone else."

Even to her own ears the words sounded harsh and bitter.

Ty turned toward her, his eyes serious. "Whatever Josh Riddley did must have been pretty bad. What happened between the two of you?"

Drawing her legs up tight against her stomach, Kara wrapped both arms around her knees. "What happened was my fault, really. I made the mistake of trusting him."

Why she was telling Ty these things puzzled her, but for some reason, be it Lane's illness, her own exhaustion or the presence of a man who'd once understood her better than anyone, she needed to talk. For once the company of a man, albeit Ty Murdock, held a kind of comfort she'd long been without. What did it matter? One of them would soon be gone, just like before.

"You still have feelings for him, don't you?"

Oh, yes, Kara still had feelings for Josh Riddley. Resentment. Fear. Guilt. "Some things never go away, Ty, no matter how much we'd like them to."

"But you've been divorced a long time."

"Not really. Even though we haven't lived together since Lane was in diapers, I didn't have the money for the divorce until about a year ago." And Josh hadn't stopped harassing her the entire time, wanting money, wanting her.

Ty was fully reclined, stretched out on the porch while Kara sat huddled inside the circle of her own arms. He rolled to one side and grasped her foot, tugging gently until she loosened her position. "Bad subject. Sorry."

"That's okay." But she uncurled her body and rose, drawing away from his warm, tempting presence. Any discussion of Josh marshaled all her defenses in a hurry and served as a reminder of why she would never fall in love again. "I'd better go check on Lane. Thanks for the cocoa."

Though Ty remained on the porch, fireflies dancing in the darkness behind him, Kara felt his coal-black gaze follow her through the living room and down the hall. As she approached her child's room, one question remained unanswered. What exactly was Ty Murdock up to?

Kara yanked her ponytail through the hole in a hot-pink bill cap and stared at her reflection in the mirror. Considering the restless night with Lane, it was a wonder she was up at all. During the few hours he'd slept, she'd stared up at the ceiling wondering about Murdock. He was being too nice, and she didn't trust him any more than she could rise and fly. Somewhere in the early morning hours when pink streaked across the eastern sky and the rooster crowed, she'd come to understand just why he'd been so pleasant. It wasn't because he was sorry for the sick child. And it wasn't because he regretted taking her family ranch. It wasn't even because he'd walked out on her six years ago. Oh, no. Murdock, the devious soul, was setting her up for the kill. He'd bring her cocoa, carry her groceries, and use that country boy charm of his to keep her off guard. He'd wear her down until she gave up and went back to Oklahoma for good.

One last glance at her sleeping son as she left the room was all she needed to stand strong against anything Murdock threw in her direction today.

"This ranch is your birthright, Lane," she whispered, "and I'll get it back for you if I have to dance with the devil himself."

Halfway to the kitchen the aroma of frying bacon slapped her in the face, slowing her steps. Dancing with the devil might come sooner than she'd expected. Murdock was still in the house. And cooking. Her heart ricocheted against her ribs. Didn't he have ranch work to do?

Stiffening her spine, she marched into the room, past the humming cowboy standing before the stove, straight to the coffee pot. Most likely he considered last night's talk a victory, but it had only been a truce brought on by exhaustion. This morning she was her old self again. And decidedly grumpy.

"'Morning, Miss Kara." Ty grinned as he turned the bacon.

Dang him. There he stood, looking good enough to eat for breakfast, barefoot, his damp, black-brown hair curling around his ears and his blue chambray shirt hanging open over a taut brown stomach, while she felt as washed-out as a pothole.

"I hope the grease burns your belly."

Ty patted the rippling stomach muscles. "Would you kiss it and make it all better?"

An image of running her tongue slowly over the brown skin formed in Kara's mind before she could stop it.

"In your dreams, cowboy." Tearing her gaze away,

she yanked a cup from the cabinet and poured a steaming stream of coffee from the pot.

"Can't blame a guy for trying."

"Leave me alone, Murdock. I've had a rough night."

At the admission, he lay the meat fork aside and looked her over, taking in the red eyes and pale complexion she'd seen in the mirror. His expression grew serious. "How's your boy?"

The concern was almost as alluring as his body.

"Right now he's mercifully asleep. But we were up and down all night."

"I know." He reached into the cabinet for a plate, spreading a paper towel on it. "I heard you."

She dumped two spoons of sugar into the cup and stirred. "Don't tell me you stayed up all night worrying about getting the chicken pox."

"Hmm?" He frowned as he flipped the crispy bacon onto the plate. "Oh, yeah. That," he said as though he'd forgotten. "I called Mom."

"Well?"

"I haven't had them."

Coffee cup halfway to her lips, Kara paused and grinned. "That's the best news I've had in three days."

He pretended hurt, then brightened. "Look at it this way. If I get sick, you'll have to take care of me."

"If you get sick, I'll let you die."

"Chicken pox aren't fatal."

"More's the pity."

He slid a bowl of country brown eggs from the refrigerator. "How do you want your eggs?"

"I'm not hungry." The last thing she wanted was to spend an entire meal sitting across from him. Last night had been all too cozy, and her mind still reeled with confusion. He'd been nice to her the day he left, too, which just proved what a pitiful judge of character she was.

"Scrambled." He cracked the eggs against the side of a bowl as if she hadn't spoken. "With picante. And I'll make extra for Lane. A sick boy needs a hearty breakfast."

"Lane's idea of a big breakfast is two strawberry Pop-Tarts. This morning I doubt if he'll want a thing."

Glancing up from his vigorous egg beating, Ty pointed a drippy fork at her. "This morning he'll have bacon and eggs."

She sighed in surrender. Let him find out the hard way that no one could force a sick five-year-old to eat. "Should I make toast?"

He nudged his chin in the direction of the oven. "Biscuits are cooking."

"When did you learn to make biscuits?" She gave him an "I ain't believing this" look.

"Anyone can do it," he answered with a grin. "Pull that little paper around the can, pop those suckers on a pan, and voilà, you got biscuits."

If she hadn't been so determined to hate his guts, she would have returned his grin. But she knew his plan. Charm absolutely oozed from his pores this morning. Why, if she didn't watch him, he'd be chasing her around the table, making cute remarks and flashing those suntanned pecs until she succumbed to... She didn't even want to think about that. Tightening her resolve, she scuttled past him to the refrigerator and the orange juice. Ty was sprinkling cheese on the steaming eggs.

"A regular Julia Child, aren't you?"

He peeked at her over one shoulder. "Who?"

This time she did grin. "Never mind."

Kara set the table. Ty followed with the bacon and a yellow mountain of scrambled eggs. As they jockeyed for position around the small kitchen, Ty's front brushed her back. Her belly clenched, and she practically fell into her chair to escape the incredible surge of energy that shot through her. She simply had to get him out of here.

Fueled by sheer determination, she plowed into a plate piled with more food than she'd eaten since...well, since yesterday when Sally had cooked lunch.

"So, when are you leaving?" She asked with false sweetness once she'd found her voice.

Ty shook an outrageous amount of hot sauce onto his eggs. "I was about to ask you the same question."

"Easy." With the slight lift of one shoulder, she tried to convey a confidence she didn't feel. "When you have the deed transferred back into Daddy's name."

The picante bottle clomped against the tabletop. Ty gave her a jaunty grin. "Then I'd say we got us a Mexican standoff."

He wasn't going to make this easy. They ate in silence for a bit while she tried to figure out a way to break the impasse.

"Is there anything I can do to make you change your mind?" Instantly she regretted the bad choice of words.

"Let's see." Mischief sparkled on Ty's face. "I won it in a poker game. Maybe..." He snapped his fingers. "I've got it." His gaze drifted over her, slow and lazy, burning its way down like a shot of brandy on a cold night. "You and I can play a little game of strip poker. Winner take all."

A hunk of biscuit lodged in her throat. She had to swallow twice to get it down. A clothed Ty Murdock was tempting enough. The thought of his dark, athletic body unclothed sent little shivers clear to her toes. The memory surfaced of the two of them, their bodies hot and slick and sated. She shoved it aside. Sex had never been their problem.

"You're dreaming again, cowboy."

"Well, in that case," he said, pushing his plate to one side, "I have another proposition for you." Scooting his chair back from the table, Ty crossed one boot over a knee and speared her with those black eyes. He suddenly looked way too serious for comfort. A playful, sexy Murdock she could handle. The serious one unsettled her.

"If it has anything to do with taking off our clothes, I'll pass."

He held his palm up like a stop sign. "Hear me out. You might even like this." Though his lips tilted in a teasing smile, there was an intensity, an energy behind it that Kara couldn't comprehend. She had a feeling she was about to find out what he was up to.

With a disbelieving huff, she tossed her head and prepared for combat. Nothing Ty Murdock proposed would get to her again.

"What if I said I'd be willing to make your son my heir?"

In one deep gasp, Kara sucked in half the air in the room, choked by the sudden fear that Ty knew about Lane. She grabbed for her juice glass and swigged, struggling to keep her face bland and her hand steady. "What did you say?"

"I've been doing a lot of thinking about this whole situation. Lane is Pete's grandson. He *should* eventually inherit this ranch if he wants it."

"Then sign it over to me."

"Hold on. I'm not finished." Ty's body was relaxed, but his expression was watchful. "Bring Lane here to live permanently. Let me see if he has what it takes to run a ranch."

"He's only five years old."

"Blood will tell."

A new shaft of fear jabbed at her. "What does that mean?" The words came out high and squeaky.

"Does he take after you? Or his father? If he's a Taylor through and through, he'll take to ranching like a bronc to bucking. I'm willing to give him that chance."

This was nuts. Why would Ty even consider such a crazy thing? Unless…but no, there was no way he could possibly know the truth about Lane. She'd given up too much to protect the secret. "I have a business to run."

"Sell it."

She snorted. "And how am I supposed to support my son?"

"That's the other part of my proposition."

Ty tilted his chair, balancing on the back two legs. Some disturbing emotion lurked in his eyes—something Kara couldn't quite identify. All her instinctive, warning bells started clamoring.

Ty slowly settled his chair back into place and leaned across the table. For once there was no laughter in his face. In fact, he looked so sincere, it scared her even more. Wrapping long brown fingers around her free hand, he said, "I want you to be my partner, Kara, just like we always planned. I want you to marry me."

If he'd asked her to ride naked in the Fourth of July Parade, she couldn't have been more shocked. The biscuit dangling limply from one hand thudded onto her plate.

"You've been thrown on your head one too many times, Bubba." A shaky voice belied the flippant words. She rubbed at the top of her hand. His touch still sizzled there like this morning's bacon, and the heat of unmet needs seared her soul. A long time ago, he'd burned her and no matter how tempting he was, she wouldn't be his fool again.

Heels of his hands resting on the tabletop, Ty lifted his fingers, then slapped them down again. "No doubt you're right about that one, but it's still what I want to do. A boy shouldn't be without a father, so if he seems taken with the cowboy way, I'll adopt him and make him my heir."

"I don't understand this." Blood pounded in her ears.

"Do you want the ranch or not?"

Fear coiled in her belly like a rattlesnake. What was he after? "Why would you do such a thing? You don't even know Lane."

"Maybe I owe you one."

"Maybe? Ha! You owe me a lot more than one."

"You're right. I do." He grinned, slow and easy, letting his gaze drift over her in a way that set her belly to quivering again with something much different than fear. "Be mighty glad to start payback any time you say."

"This is nuts." As nervous as a wild bronc, she jerked out of her chair and began gathering plates and forks. He wanted to marry her and adopt her son? If it hadn't been so sad, she would have laughed. Could a man adopt his own son?

A long time ago she'd fantasized this very scene, only it had been filled with love, not IOUs. That Ty actually had a conscience gave her some comfort, but there was no love between them now and certainly no trust.

She thrust the dirty dishes onto the bar, then went around to pull them through to the kitchen side. Ty remained in his chair, staring at her across the counter, his expression so sincere Kara's knees quaked.

"It's the only solution, Kara. I'll keep the ranch, build it up, prosper from it, and you'll be securing it for Lane's future. Otherwise, it's mine alone, and you and Lane are out on your ear."

"There has to be more to it than that." Her mind worked frantically.

"Okay. I'll admit it's crossed my mind that nobody believes a Murdock can settle down. I aim to prove them wrong."

Her shaky hands gripped the bar. Ty wanted to marry her and make Lane his heir out of some neurotic need to redeem the Murdock name?

"And what if you change your mind and don't stay?" Ty's boots had been under so many beds, she couldn't imagine him being around long.

He shrugged. "I'll give you a divorce, but the ranch is Lane's, no strings attached."

Something about his reasoning was off center, but she couldn't quite figure it out. Since the moment she'd walked back in this house, she'd not been thinking rationally, and now it was even worse. He was manipulating her; that was it. This devil in cowboy boots knew her back was against the wall, that she had no legal recourse, no way to fight him and win. So he'd decided to dangle a carrot in front of her, certain she'd never agree to such an outrageous deal. He expected her to refuse, to go skulking back to the city with her sick child in tow while he stayed behind, grew rich and fat on what was rightfully hers, all with a clear conscience. He could tell himself and the whole world that he'd tried to do right by her and she'd turned him down.

The snake. She wiped sweaty hands down the side of her jeans and steadied herself. The slimy son of a serpent. He was gambling on her refusal. Well, she'd done a little poker playing in her life, too, and this time she'd call his bluff.

She marched around the end of the bar, clapped a hand on each hip, and gave him the stubborn thrust of her jaw.

"Murdock," she swallowed the lump that threatened to choke her. "This is my family's ranch. And if it takes marrying the lowest form of life on the planet to keep it, I'll do it. You just got yourself a wife."

Chapter Seven

Rounding the corner inside the barn, Kara heard Ty quietly talking. Hay rustled and bodies shifted behind the wall.

"Come on, baby. That's it. I know you want it."

Kara's mouth went dry as her imagination went wild. It was bad enough to have him flaunting his rock-hard athlete's body in front of her day and night, purposely standing too close and parading around the house without a shirt. Even her dreams had been fraught with images of frantic lovemaking followed by the horror of Ty driving away in a red pickup. Now, she had to stand here and listen to him seduce some woman in her own barn.

A few days ago he'd proposed a marriage of convenience and for the sake of her family home she had agreed to marry him as soon as Lane was feeling better. They'd even managed to spend some time working together without killing each other. But even a marriage of convenience deserved a certain amount of respect. She wasn't about to let him get away with barn stall trysts.

Wrenching the door open, she barged in, prepared to see naked bodies scramble for clothes. What she actually saw was Ty crouched in front of a new calf, teaching it to drink from a bottle while he murmured gentle encouragement.

Feeling positively ridiculous, she went weak with relief, but the images in her mind wouldn't go away. Her body felt flushed and heavy, desire dancing around the edges, a feeling that infuriated her. Hadn't she learned the hard way that runaway desire has far-reaching consequences?

"Got us another motherless calf." A worry line between his brows, Ty peered over one shoulder, oblivious to her train of thought. "That makes four to hand feed. We're losing too many mamas."

"Wonder why?" With great effort, Kara concentrated on the troubling situation, though her thoughts kept straying to the way Ty's white T-shirt pulled up from the band of his jeans, exposing a narrow strip of dark skin.

Since her arrival, she'd discovered many problems around the place. The cattle breeding program was off schedule, fences and barns were in disrepair, stalls needed cleaning and none of the spring calves had been worked.

"Some of these cows are too old for breeding. We need to cull them out, separate the calves, band them, brand them, medicate them. You know, the things that should be done in spring." All the while he spoke, Ty gripped the oversize baby bottle in one hand and stroked the small red calf with the other. Hooves splayed for balance, the calf sucked rhythmically, the foamy milk replacer dribbling from the corners of his mouth.

"I'll do anything I can to help."

"You sure?" Ty glanced up at her.

She nodded, annoyed that he would ask such a thing. "This is my ranch. I'll do whatever's necessary to make it prosper."

"Well, in that case." His ornery, twinkling gaze flowed over her freshly washed jeans, white camp blouse and virgin boots. "Grab a shovel. We're mucking out the barns today."

While Ty laughed at Kara's reaction, the motherless calf took one mighty suck on the bottle, then butted Ty right in the chest, knocking him on his backside. His hat landed in a fresh pile of the aforementioned muck.

Kara burst out laughing. She loved that calf.

Hours later, with sweat and grime and bits of moldy hay covering every thread of clothing, Kara scooped the last shovelful into the wheelbarrow.

"We make a great team, don't you think?" Ty leaned his shovel against the back of the stall.

If she answered honestly, Kara would have to admit they did. With her dad and Sally keeping an eye on Lane, Kara had made frequent checks on the sick boy and still managed to assist Ty with some badly needed work on the crumbling ranch. Their morning together had gone surprisingly well. Ty had kept up a running dialogue of wisecracks, and in spite of her misgivings, she'd laughed and joked in return.

Ty crossed to where she stood and plucked a bit of straw from her shoulder. Considering last night's dreams and her irrational thoughts this morning, Kara grew warm all over.

"You have, uh..." He pointed at the front of her blouse where a green caterpillar inched down one breast. "Let me get that for you."

Whipping off a leather glove faster than she could react, Ty reached for the caterpillar, his fingers lightly grazing the rise of Kara's breast.

She squealed and jumped back, slapping at her chest until the offending creature went flying across the stall.

"I would have been much gentler." Ty wagged his eyebrows up and down. "Much."

"You're such a thoughtful guy, Murdock," she answered sarcastically.

"I knew you'd be impressed." He reached around and brushed dirt from the back of her jeans. He just couldn't help himself. Getting her mad, in a teasing kind of way, was so much fun. He ducked when she grabbed the shovel and swung at him, grinning in mock fury. They really were a good team, and they were making progress, though he was hard-pressed to make her see that. Yet.

"Hands off the merchandise, Murdock." She made another foray at him. Muck fell from the shovel.

"What, no roll in the hay? No samples before the wedding?" Lord knew, he was sorely tempted.

Laughing at her mutinous expression, he took the wheelbarrow handle and started outside. Kara followed with the shovels.

"Looks like somebody's coming." A rooster tail of dust rose behind a brown postal truck barreling beneath the Star M sign. Ty's joking mood vanished as he realized what was about to happen. "Let's go see what it is."

"Dad can get it."

"No. Let's do it."

Expression puzzled, Kara propped the shovels against the barn. "What's going on, Murdock?"

"Now don't get all defensive. Just come see." With a mixture of excitement and dread, Ty grabbed her hand and pulled her toward the approaching truck. For a moment he thought she would pull away, but, to his relief, she came, letting him hold her hand as they jogged toward the house.

When they'd received the box and signed for it, Kara studied the address on the cover. "This is from my shop."

"Open it." Ty suddenly felt more nervous than he had been the first time he'd ridden in competition.

"No. You open it." To his dismay she shoved the box at him, her face riddled with anxiety. "I have a feeling you know what's in here."

Gently he tugged her down on the porch and laid the box in her lap. "Open it. Please."

Stuffing his gloves in a back pocket, he knelt on one knee, waiting, hoping.

Curiosity won out. She unwrapped the package and lifted the lid. Ty's heart thudded unevenly.

As she peeled away the tissue paper inside, she gasped and looked up at him, eyes wide, face pale. Her throat worked spasmodically, a dozen emotions playing across her face as she lifted the delicate lace wedding dress from the box.

"You did this?" Her voice shook and Ty wondered why.

"Do you like it?" He didn't normally feel this anxious about anything, and it scared him.

With trembling fingers, she dropped the dress into the box. Her breath came short and fast. "Send it back."

His heart plummeted. "We're getting married, Kara," he said gently. "I want you to have a beautiful dress."

"Why are you doing this?" Her eyes glistened suspiciously. Jiminy Christmas was she fixing to cry?

Ty was bewildered. He'd known she would pitch her usual fit, but he hadn't expected her to look scared. No longer able to resist the urge, he touched her, stroking loose strands of hair away from her cheeks. "It's our wedding, darlin'. I want it to be special for both of us."

Kara sprang from his touch, her face set. "What are you trying to do, Ty? This isn't a real wedding. This is a business deal. You don't love me, and I *sure* don't love you."

Bounding off the porch, she sprinted toward the barn, leaving Ty alone with a lacy garment as delicate and creamy as Kara's skin. He rubbed the back of his neck and looked heavenward. So much for thinking they'd made some progress.

If she didn't like the dress, she was gonna hate the wedding.

"This is insane, Murdock." Kara kicked at the back step with her new white lace-up boots...the ones he'd ordered to go with the dress.

Ty leaned against a porch post looking as relaxed as a dead snake. He also looked gorgeous in a short tuxedo jacket, white shirt and black jeans, an outfit as absolutely out of place at a marriage of convenience as the incredible lace creation she wore.

"Did you, or did you not, tell me to plan the wedding?"

"Not like this." Panic gripped her. "I thought it

would just be you and me and the judge down at the courthouse.''

Without her consent and against her wishes, Ty had invited half the countryside to a full-fledged Western-style wedding, complete with mounted wedding party. In a whirlwind of activity he'd arranged the kind of affair they'd planned together one summer night a life-time ago.

To make matters worse, Marietta, whom she'd considered an ally, had turned traitor the moment she'd arrived from Oklahoma City.

"Wear the dress, Kara.'' Marietta held up the magnificent creation, tempting her. "What harm could there be in that?''

"Ty bought it. I don't want him thinking that I've changed my mind.''

"About what?''

"Him.'' She waved her arms like a drowning victim. "All of this. I'm certain he has something up his sleeve, but I haven't figured out what it could be.''

"Did you ever think maybe the cowboy is sincere? Girl, you didn't hear his voice when he phoned to order that dress, and from the way his eyes follow you, I think the man is in love.''

Kara huffed derisively. "The only person he loves is himself.''

"I think he's changed, Kara. And besides, your cowboy is hotter than the face of the sun.'' Grinning, she fanned herself. "That face and body could make a girl forget a lot of things.''

"I won't ever forget the torture he put me through. I don't love him. I won't love him.'' Love made one vulnerable.

"Fine, then, but I helped choose this dress because

I knew you loved it, and you're wearing it today if I have to hog-tie you and dress you myself.''

So, here Kara stood, wearing an outfit she adored, with the man she'd once loved more than was prudent, wondering how she'd get through the evening with her resolutions firmly in place. Being with Ty, day in and day out, was starting to wear her down. She'd been alone too long, and having a sexy cowboy lavish such attention on her made her ache in ways she had to ignore.

"We planned this wedding a long time ago, Kara.'' Ty pushed away from the porch and went to check the saddle cinches one last time. "I thought you'd be tickled.''

"Ticked, Murdock, not tickled. We made a lot of plans together, all of which you walked away from, I might add. Why would you choose to honor this one?''

After a sharp tug on the cinch, he looked over one shoulder, his lips tilting in a smile. "Just a sentimental fool, I guess.''

"Fool is the operative word.''

Ty stood, dusted off his hands and laced his fingers together, offering her a leg up.

"I can't do it. Not this way.'' Kara whirled and started toward the back door, the pointed lace hem swishing around her boots. "Go down there and tell everyone that the wedding is off.''

"Are you ready to give up the ranch? *And* embarrass your daddy in front of all his friends?''

She stopped dead in her tracks and pivoted. Blackmail. He was using blackmail. Her daddy had practically tap-danced on the roof, arthritic knee and all, when they'd told him the news. He'd been so happy, that she hadn't had the heart to admit the whole thing was a sham. He'd find out soon enough. But if she let him down now, in front of his friends, he'd never get over it. And Lane would lose his birthright.

She could keep her distance. She had to...for Lane.

Resigned, Kara started toward the waiting horse. Ty stood there watching her with those black eyes as she moved across the grass. His unwavering gaze captured every sway and movement of her body. A curl of recognition fluttered in her belly. Ty had the uncanny ability to caress with his eyes and make her feel like the sexiest woman alive. Lord, help her. She couldn't give in to this insanity.

When she reached him, instead of assisting her to mount, he wrapped a hand around each of her arms and stared down at her with enough sincerity to convince a twelve-man jury that he would never so much as tell a white lie.

A quiver of nerves shimmered through her at his nearness. After two weeks of having him underfoot day and night, reminding her of all that was missing in her life, it was getting harder and harder to keep an emotional distance. And how could any woman not feel emotional on her wedding day?

"You look very beautiful, Kara." Ty's voice was unexpectedly soft and husky, his hands warm through the sheer material of her blouse.

She *felt* beautiful in the long, swirling skirt of rich cream lace with its exquisitely beaded bodice and lace-edged handkerchief hem.

Goose bumps shivered up her spine, her mouth suddenly dry. Mesmerized by the sincerity in his voice, the heat in his eyes, she licked her lips. Ty took that as an invitation. With slow certainty, he pulled her close and lowered his head, bumping her forehead with the brim of his best black Stetson. She hardly noticed, so intent was she on the woodsy smell of his cologne, the moist heat of his breath, the firm curve of his lips as they closed over hers.

The kiss lasted only a few seconds, a mere meeting of mouths, a soft brushing of skin against skin. But the ripple of desire purling in her stomach lasted much longer. Mellowed by his gentleness, she laid her head against his chest and sighed.

He'd been like this for days, wearing away at her resistance with his teasing and his kindness and his simmering looks. Even though she'd scorned the wedding dress, refusing to touch it until Marietta arrived, he'd gone right on playing the loving bridegroom.

After today she'd have to renew her defenses. But not today. Today she was getting married. Charade or not, a teeny-tiny part of her wanted to pretend it was real. Just this once, she would play his game.

Ty smoothed one hand down the back of her hair, his hand lingering on her bare shoulders. She shivered anew at the sensuous yearnings his touch elicited.

"The guests are waiting," his soft voice urged.

Afraid to speak, lest her voice quiver like her belly, she stepped back, nodding her consent. Her emotions frightened her. She'd once been a marshmallow in his hands, succumbing to a few seductive words and caresses, and she simply could not chance that happening again.

Ty circled her waist with both hands, lifting her easily into the saddle. Watching her, holding her eyes with his, he let his hand linger, drifting down her thigh, cupping her calf seductively as he placed her foot in the stirrup. Kara swallowed hard and took the reins.

Taffy, decked out like a parade mount, shifted beneath the weight, tossed her beribboned head and started forward.

As they made their way across the open pasture, the air was alive with the sights and sounds of late spring. Butterflies flitted over a profusion of wildflowers, whose gentle fragrance wafted upward with every footfall of the horses. Texas bluebonnets swayed in the breeze, nodding their royal-blue heads as the riders passed. The setting was perfect, idyllic. How could something so wrong feel so right?

In a tangle of sensual awareness, they rode in silence toward the tree-lined creek. She knew where they were going. Had known as surely as the mare had known. Kara glanced toward the man riding beside her and then back to the crowd gathering beneath the natural arch of trees leading down to the creek. Did he remember what this place had once meant to them?

Of course he did. He had to.

Kara sat up straighter in the saddle and mentally shook herself, battling against the sweet pull of the past. Knowing Ty Murdock, he'd chosen this particular spot with the sole purpose of rubbing salt in an old wound, a kind of psychological one-upmanship. Here he'd taken her innocence and stolen her heart.

"Do you like the braid?"

Kara's head snapped around, her thoughts befuddled. She stared mutely for several seconds before understanding dawned. Her mare's mane was painstakingly braided with fronds of delicate white flowers intertwined with sky-blue ribbons.

So Ty was the one who'd gone to all that trouble.

"It's beautiful," she answered truthfully, the purl of pleasure starting up again. How was she supposed to remain aloof when he kept playing the solicitous lover?

"There's your dad."

Coming toward them on his favorite gelding, Pete looked like the proverbial cat that ate the canary.

"You two ready?" He circled his prancing buckskin to stand alongside Kara.

The jitters came back...and brought their friends. "As ready as I'll ever be."

Pete shot Kara a puzzled look, then patted her hand and winked. "No need to be nervous. The two of you shoulda done this years ago."

She hoped he'd never discover how close to the truth he'd come.

Three abreast, with Kara in the center, they rode onward to the waiting crowd.

The knot of tension in Kara's belly wound tighter and tighter. She hadn't expected it to be this scary. Maybe she should have tried harder to find another solution. What if he discovered the truth about Lane? What if her father found out and disowned them both forever? What if Ty expected more out of this marriage than she was willing to give?

If she hadn't been pinned in by Ty and Pete, she'd have bolted. But before she could find a way of escape, she was there, standing in front of a bale of hay with Ty on one side and her father on the other.

"You sure look pretty, Mama."

The childlike whisper from her son was reminder enough of who really mattered in all this. Clutching the ring box in one hand, Lane grinned up at her, his sweet face still bearing the marks of his recent bout with chicken pox. Kara's heart twisted with a love so fierce she knew she'd do anything to secure this child's future.

"You're looking mighty handsome yourself there, cowboy," she whispered back, bending for a quick kiss before turning her attention to the minister. He stood behind the hay bale, his leathery hands holding the white Bible her mother had given her for Christmas when she was twelve. Now, where had he gotten that?

"Are we ready to begin?" The rodeo preacher stepped forward, his gentle eyes questioning.

A surge of pure terror shot through her. Ready? How could she be ready? She was about to jump feet-first into a volcano.

Marietta pushed a nosegay of bluebonnets into her hands. Then, glancing at Kara's handsome groom, she raised her perfectly penciled brows and smiled.

Kara relaxed ever so slightly and scanned the gathering. Good solid country folks she'd known forever stood with smiles on their faces, clearly delighted at the turn of events. Her gaze fell to her father, standing on her left, straight and proud in his new Western duds, fairly glowing with pleasure. Last of all, she looked down at the child. Lane deserved to know these people, to grow up in the secure, country strength of neighbors who'd known his ancestors forever. Neighbors who would lend a hand in hard times, who'd help you celebrate the good times. Lane belonged here, just as she did. If it took marrying Ty Murdock to make it happen, so be it.

Another sweep of the crowd and she saw Ty's sister Jolene surrounded by four unkempt children. She looked tired and wan and ten years older than Kara knew her to be. Her latest husband was nowhere in sight. Poor Jolene. She was a perfect example of what happened to a woman who loved the wrong kind of man. Kara was determined not to let that happen to her. She could marry Ty, but she would never again let him have her heart.

Taking a deep steady breath, Kara nodded her readiness, and the ceremony began. The old cowboy reverend surprised her with his eloquence as he talked of God's timing and the spiritual power of love between a man and a woman. It was the last thing she wanted or expected to hear, but as the minister's hushed voice filled the air, the whole of nature felt in balance.

A gentle rustling breeze stirred the spring-scented meadow as a pair of bluebirds darted through the trees, their streak of color matching the carpet of Texas Bluebonnets. In the background rose the happy murmur of water as the rain-filled creek tumbled over rocks.

Kara fought against the surreal air hanging over the wedding. The ceremony was beautiful, perfect, exactly the way she'd wanted her wedding to be, and the notion moved her to unbearable sadness. She was too wise to believe in fairy tales.

"Do you, Kara, take this man, Tyler, to be your lawfully wedded husband? To love, honor and cherish, as long as you both shall live?"

A frightful trembling started deep in her soul and worked its way into her knees. What was she doing? How could she lie about something so sacred and ever expect things to turn out all right?

She glanced at her father and then at her son, their faces alight with happiness, and tamped back the hysteria. She had to do this. For them.

Ty must have sensed her misgivings because he chose that moment to slide a strong arm around her waist, steadying her. He shifted in her direction. Compelled, Kara lifted her gaze to his. He winked, the hint of a smile settling around his lips. A chink of her armor fell away.

"I do," she answered, surprised that the words came out a breathy whisper, worthy of a loving bride.

Then came Ty's turn. His black gaze never left her face as he spoke his own vows. Had she not known the whole thing was a charade, she would have believed every word. As it was, a seed of pleasure sprouted upward, and Kara found herself fighting not to embrace the beautiful dream.

"Are there rings?" the preacher asked.

Another surprise awaited Kara. Propelled by his grandfather, Lane stepped forward with a blue velvet box holding two matching gold bands sprinkled with star-shaped diamonds. She hadn't even considered the rings, and she certainly hadn't expected anything more than a cheap band to make things official. Why had Ty gone to such trouble and expense for a make-believe marriage? And why had he chosen a ring for himself?

At the moment she couldn't think straight enough to worry about it. Following Ty's lead, she took his warm hand in her trembling one and exchanged bands. When she felt him tremble, too, Kara almost lost her nerve.

The preacher's next words jump-started her heart.

"I now pronounce you husband and wife."

Husband and wife. The words bounced around inside her head. She was married. To Ty Murdock. She gulped down a surge of foreboding and stood frozen, staring down at the masculine hand holding hers. In the next instant Ty wrapped his arms around her, and she forgot everything as he kissed her senseless. When he pulled away, laughing down at her stunned expression, the rest of the gathering reacted. At least fifty cowboy hats took flight as a collective whoop of celebration broke across the meadow.

Ty stood in a crowd of well-wishers listening to the ranchers' usual worries of drought and falling livestock prices. He smiled and responded in all the right places, though his mind was on his new wife as she moved about the open-air tent playing the gracious hostess to folks she'd known forever.

He'd managed to get Kara to the altar, but now he wondered where to go from here. She clearly resented it, still holding a grudge against him after all this time.

He recalled the moment before the ceremony when he'd told her she was beautiful. Just for that brief interval the old Kara had returned. Then she'd caught herself and erected that wall of reserve again, something she did every time he got too close.

His gaze fell to the small boy playing around Pete's feet. That was another place he'd have to step easy. Whenever Ty had visited the sick room, Lane had watched him, wary and silent. When his mama came around he lit up like a sunrise and was as cute as a new pup.

"Mighty nice weddin', Ty." Jess Martin, Ty's best man and former traveling partner, clapped him on the shoulder. The smell of barbecue welled up from the plate he carried.

"Downright romantic, if you ask me," Sally said as she and Pete joined the circle of friends.

"Who'da believed Sam Murdock's son would ever make a husband." This from a sharp-eyed old biddy standing beside Pete and Sally. "Why, I remember the way Sam ran after every—"

"Mildred," Sally cut in. "This boy is not his daddy."

For a tense moment, Ty stared at the old woman and fought the terrible notion that she was right. What if he couldn't stay faithful? What if he got up one morning and drove away just like his daddy had done?

Desperately he searched the crowd for Kara. Catching sight of her, some of his tension eased. He could do this. Fact of the business, he wanted to. For Kara. No old gossip was going to spoil his wedding.

Kara tilted her head and laughed. Mesmerized by the curve of her neck and the sparkling rhinestones dangling from her ears, Ty dismissed the woman's comments. The garland of flowers Marietta had woven into Kara's blond hair fell to the side and swished across her small shoulder. His stomach lifted at the sight, desire rising in him. She was his wife. At least for now.

Without taking his eyes off her, he set down his champagne flute and started toward her. This party was over. He was ready to take his new bride home.

"I'll take Lane back to the motel with me for the night," Marietta offered.

Under the pretense of refilling their empty plates, the two friends had managed to edge away from the crowd long enough for a private chat.

Kara fidgeted with the ring that felt so foreign on her hand. "What for?"

"You've just married one of the hottest men I've

ever laid eyes on." Marietta gave Kara's shoulder an exasperated nudge. "This is your wedding night, girl."

"I'm not *sleeping* with him," Kara hissed, slanting a look toward the gorgeous cowboy weaving his way across the crowded tent. Her pulse did a stutter step. "This is a business deal."

Marietta arched a skeptical eyebrow. "Well, honey, from the looks your new husband's been giving you all afternoon, I think business is the last thing on his mind."

Kara remembered those looks, but she also remembered a nineteen-year-old girl alone in a strange city with the result of Ty's passion inside her. Her body might want him, did want him, if she admitted it, but her body had misled her before. Ty might sleep with her tonight and be gone in the morning.

"All the more reason for Lane to stay right here with me where he belongs." Plopping her plate on the nearest table, she scanned the crowd. The boy had wondered off in search of his granddad, and Kara was relieved to see him pulling on her father's pant leg. They made an endearing sight, the old rancher and the five-year-old dressed to the nines in matching Western wear, right down to black-yoked jackets and shiny, silver belt buckles.

"I don't think this is going to be as easy as you think," Marietta warned, drawing Kara's attention back to the problem of her new husband. "What if he discovers Lane is his son?"

"He won't."

"What about Josh? If he finds out you've remarried, he'll make trouble. You know he will."

Kara forgot to breathe. She hadn't considered Josh.

He was cruel enough to make her life more miserable than he already had. Fortunately, he wasn't yet aware of her marriage. Until Lane was the legal owner of this ranch, she'd have to be very careful that he didn't find out.

"All I care about is my son and what's rightfully his. Don't you worry your pretty red head," she said with forced confidence. "You distract Josh. I can handle Murdock."

"Then, get to handling, girl, because here he comes." Marietta focused her bright smile on Ty. "Lovely wedding, Ty."

"Yeah." He gave her the benefit of a quick grin, then turned his gaze to Kara. "Ready to go?"

"Where?"

"Home."

Kara was exhausted and more than a little ready to get away from all these well-meaning friends. Pretending to be the happy bride was starting to wear thin, and Ty would be much easier to handle in private. Most important, once they were back at the house, they could end this charade.

"Let me get Lane, and I'll be ready." Kara turned to go after him. Ty's hand on her arm stopped her.

"Pete's taking him."

"No, he isn't." Kara fought the urge to scream.

"Sure is. I just came from that direction and the little guy is all excited about spending the night with his granddad."

"You had no right to do that," Kara said stiffly.

"It was Pete's idea."

"Well, I'm sorry. I want him home with me."

"Don't spoil their fun, Kara. It's important to your dad."

Great. He was using her father and son against her when she knew very well it was his own fun he didn't want spoiled. She had news for him. With or without Lane in the house, there wasn't going to be any monkey business. Sharing her body might be tempting but the reminder of their last time together would always keep her in control. With a huff of surrender, Kara said, "Let's go, then."

"Jess is bringing up the horse."

"Where's Taffy?" Kara looked around for the mare, but saw only Ty's big roan gelding.

"Jess will ride her back to the barn."

She threw her palms up. "And how am I suppose to get home?"

"On Cochise." He nodded toward his own mount. "With me."

"No. That's silly." But a wayward longing rose at the thought of snuggling close to Ty on the ride home. Already the faint scent of him, the sight of his dark skin against the snowy shirt and the sound of his warm baritone tormented her overwrought senses.

"It's symbolic." A smile danced around Ty's enchanting lips. "We rode in as two, and we'll ride out as one."

Shades of yesterday. How had he remembered the childish, overly sentimental plans they'd made beneath the stars all those years ago?

"I won't do it." Shaking her head, she backed away.

"I'll make a scene." Mischief glittered in his dark eyes as he came toward her slowly, like a coyote stalking its prey.

Both titillated and annoyed, she halted, the swishing

lace of her gown sensitizing her calves. "You wouldn't."

"Sure I would."

He would, the devil. He loved being the center of attention. He'd like nothing better than to throw her over the saddle and ride off laughing and waving his hat, delighted to carry her kicking and screaming back to the house.

With an exaggerated sigh, she gave up and started toward the waiting horse. Might as well get this over with. As she brushed past him, Ty grabbed her arm and pulled her back, whispering down into her startled face. Little tremors of anticipation shimmied through her.

"Gotta give the guests what they came for."

Oh, dang. She tingled all over at the thought.

Sweeping her dramatically into his arms, Ty lowered his head, bringing his mouth within millimeters of hers. Kara braced herself for an earth-shattering kiss.

"Lay a good 'un on her, Ty."

Double dang. They had an audience—a whole herd of grinning cowboys.

Ty's lips moved closer until his warm, champagne-scented breath mingled with her own. Her heart skipped a beat.

Just when she was certain she would be vaporized by her own anticipation, Ty swooped down and rubbed his nose back and forth over hers in an Eskimo kiss.

"Thought I was gonna kiss you again, didn't you?" he asked, the devil's own mischief alight in his eyes.

Laughter broke out around them. In spite of her resolve not to fall for his charm, she wanted to laugh with them.

She rolled her eyes instead.

"Oh, go ahead and laugh. It'll do you good."

"I hate you," she said, but her smile betrayed her.

As though he'd never heard anything so funny, Ty threw back his head and roared. He settled her on her feet, stuck a boot in the stirrup and mounted Cochise. Reaching down, he grasped Kara's arms and lifted her easily into the spot behind his saddle.

He tipped his Stetson to the crowd. "Thank ya'll for coming. We'll see ya as soon as we come up for air."

Kara gasped, turned beet red and hid her face against her husband's broad back. As they rode away amid the hoots, cheers and laughter, one thing was clear, everyone at the wedding believed it was real. For a few seconds, there, she'd wanted to believe it herself.

Chapter Eight

"I've got some champagne on ice in the bedroom."
Ty whisked off his tie and shed the fancy tux jacket.

With her arms crossed protectively over her chest,
Kara stood in the too-quiet living room, facing the
moment she'd dreaded since the day they'd made this
crazy agreement. Ty Murdock, looking dark and de-
lectable, stared at her as if she was a hot cinnamon
roll, while he slowly unfastened the single row of but-
tons on his gleaming white shirt.

"You'd rather take a nice bubble bath first?" He
arched an eyebrow, teasing. "Together?"

All the way home from the wedding celebration,
she'd been pressed close to the muscles of Ty's strong
back, her arms wrapped around his waist. By the time
he'd lifted her down from the horse, she was pulsating
with the need to throw herself into his arms and make
this wedding night real. Marietta was right. This was
not going to be easy.

She licked her suddenly dry lips and forced out her answer. "No."

"I'll give you one of my famous back rubs," he coaxed, coming toward her, devilment in his smile.

She backed away, eyes glued to the naked brown chest peeking from his now unbuttoned shirt. He kept coming.

She held up a hand to stop his advance. Ty paid her no mind. He backed her into the wall, pressed a hand to the plaster behind her and moved within a whisper of touching her all over.

"It was a nice day, Ty," she started.

"It's going to be an even nicer night." His warm breath brushed across her cheek. "I like this lacy stuff." He ran a finger beneath the neckline of her dress. "I've been wanting to take it off you all day."

"No." She pushed his hand away.

"What's the matter?" He moved the offending hand to the sensitive flesh behind her ear, lightly rubbing. It was all she could do to keep from leaning into his touch. "Afraid you'll like it?"

Kara closed her eyes and shivered. She was afraid, all right. Terrified that she'd fall under his spell and suffer the consequences all over again.

"It's not what I want."

"What do you want, Kara?" His lips grazed hers. "Tell me." He kissed her again, nudging, coaxing. "Anything you want. I'm your man."

He was intentionally twisting her words, using them to seduce her. And she thought it might be working.

"That's not what I meant." The words sounded strangled.

"Are you sure?" His smooth jaw, freshly shaved for the wedding, brushed her neck as his mouth found its way to her collarbone and nibbled at the tattletale pulse.

Kara fought the wash of sensation, angry at her body's betrayal, but helpless to control it. Tingles ran down her neck and chest—wonderful, drugging ripples of pleasure. If she didn't do something to stop this soon, it would be too late.

With an enormous effort of will, Kara twisted away from his seeking lips. "Can't you take no for an answer?"

"Only if you mean it."

She gritted her teeth and repeated the "son of a serpent" chant that had kept her going for two weeks. The phrase reminded her why she was here in the first place. With trembling arms she shoved at his naked chest. "Sleeping with you was not part of the deal."

He stumbled back, his expression dubious. "I don't remember agreeing to that."

"You did."

Frowning, he pressed a finger to his temple. "Seems like a man would remember something that important."

"You have a tendency to forget important things."

Ty drew back, and Kara was almost certain a flicker of hurt came and went behind his intentionally pleasant expression. He held her gaze for an eternal moment, then shrugged and slipped into his cocky-cowboy mode.

"Well, shoot, darlin'," he drawled in his best Texas accent, "if you're going to be that way about it..." He pointed a finger at her in sudden inspiration, the ripples of chest and shoulder muscle taunting Kara's hyperactive senses. "Tell you what. You make the popcorn, and I'll dig out the Monopoly."

"Do what?" She blinked in confusion.

"When was the last time you played Monopoly?" He grinned and swung around, flashing her another view of firm brown flesh. Kara was hard-pressed not to salivate.

"I, uh..." His sudden change of mood and conversation had her completely off balance. But that was Ty. He could change direction faster than a champion cutting horse. Sometimes he did it for orneriness. Sometimes it was to hide his real feelings. Regardless of the reason this time, she hoped he choked on the popcorn.

Her insides taut with sexual tension, Kara raised cold hands to her burning cheeks and took a long, cleansing breath. She could do this. She could sit across the kitchen table from Ty Murdock and play a simple little game. If only she could get him to button his shirt.

Ty was about to die of heat stroke. If he stood here in the blazing July sun, staring at the back of Kara's bare thighs one more minute, he'd either fall over dead or yank her backward off that ladder, rip off those denim shorts and cool this hot blood pounding in his veins.

Oblivious to his thoughts, Kara waved a hammer toward the gabled peak of the old hay barn. "Look out for those wasps."

Groaning, Ty clambered up the ladder positioned beside hers and took his frustrations out on a poor hapless nail. With all the work to do around the place, he should have been too tired to lust after his own wife, but that part of his brain and body hadn't relaxed since she'd turned him down on their wedding night. That game of Monopoly had cost him dearly.

"Once we get the sheet iron nailed down, we'll be ready to paint, won't we?" The thin cotton material of Kara's blouse stretched tightly over her breasts as she turned toward him.

"Yeah," he grumbled. Panting, not painting, was on his mind. Kara's "let's be friends" attitude was a nice change from "let's kill Ty," but it came up way short of the happy-ever-after scenario swirling in his head.

Kara glanced across the shiny length of roof and raised an eyebrow. Without a lick of makeup, her nose cutely sunburned, she was the prettiest thing imaginable. She grinned at his sour expression. "Who peed in your Post Toasties this morning?"

"It's too hot to roof a sheet-metal barn." With grim satisfaction he drove another nail deep.

"It was your idea," she said pointedly. "First the barn so we can work the calves, then the cross fences."

"I know." He forced a smile and searched for his usual flip answer. Finding none, he offered, "Sorry."

His libido was not her problem. It was her fault, but it wasn't her problem.

Ty lifted a section of rusted tin and tossed it to the ground. A swarm of disturbed wasps shot out between the open trusses. He swatted, waving his arms wildly as he backed quickly down the ladder, only to catch a boot heel on the last rung. He went sprawling into the loose dirt below.

Kara yelped and scrambled down, too, but not in time to see the mess he was in. She fell in a tangle on top of him, smelling like sun and honeysuckle. It was the ideal position for what Ty had in mind, except for the blasted wasps.

With the angry insects swirling overhead, Ty circled Kara with both arms and struggled upright. Shielding her with his body, he quickly guided them to safety on the opposite side of the barn.

"I think you just saved my life," Kara panted with a grin.

"In some cultures that means you owe me—" with a fake scowl, he tapped his cheek "—what was it? Oh, yeah, I think I remember. Your body now belongs to me until you perform some incredible act that releases you from the debt." He started toward her, grinning. "I can even suggest what that incredible act might be."

A water faucet jutted from the side of the building. Kara grabbed for the attached hose, wielding it like a weapon. "Back off, cowboy. I can put out your eye at fifty paces."

"Coward," he laughed, but he stopped just the same as she turned the hose on for a much-needed drink. So far, pressing her had only made things worse.

Kara sighed with relief as the icy well water trickled down her parched throat.

"Hey, save some for me," Ty teased, and eased around to the spigot. He waited until she wasn't looking and turned it full blast. The water erupted from Kara's lips like Old Faithful. Sputtering, she jumped back, green eyes glaring at him.

"You are a son of sidewinder," she declared with amazingly good humor. Then she aimed the hose directly at his head, blowing his hat onto the dusty, manure-laden barnyard.

He stalked toward her. "Nobody messes with my hat, woman."

"Oh, yeah?" She blasted the fallen Stetson until it danced and tumbled in the dirt. "Take that."

In mock fury Ty bellowed like a bull in heat and roared toward her, dodging and sputtering as she turned the hose on him. Water spraying wildly over both of them, he captured the hose, though Kara wasn't about to give up without a fight. Water molded her shirt against heaving breasts as they wrestled. Ty was hard-pressed to remember what they were fighting over.

Ty dropped the hose, letting the water spray around their feet. "You're driving me crazy, you know that?" He backed her against the barn wall, bracing a hand on each side of her face. Her eyes went wide as the laughter died, but she didn't push him away this time. He figured this was as much cooperation as he was likely to get, so he leaned in, pressing his sodden body full length against hers. His voice grew husky. "I saw this once in a movie."

Kara jumped when she felt his hot tongue against her cool wet jaw, but she held her ground. For days now she'd been so hungry for his touch that it shamed her. Just this once, here in the open where nothing could really happen, she wanted to give in. To feel Ty's rock-hard body against hers. To stroke the muscles of his chest and back. To taste the heat and salt of his mouth.

Ty's tongue traced a single drop of water to her lips, paused at the corner of her mouth, suspended, waiting for a signal from her. She was drowning, going under for the last time. Her pulse thundered. Ty's echoed. *Now,* she thought. *Kiss me, now.*

Suddenly all desire fled in a blinding stab of pain. She shrieked and jerked away, slapping frantically at her leg. A red wasp circled her thigh.

"He stung me!" she cried into Ty's baffled face.

"Oh, baby." He fell to his knees. Though his breath still came in raspy gasps, hot against the sensitive tissue inside her thigh, he was instantly focused on her injury. His hands were gentle as they probed the spot. When he pressed a tender kiss against the throbbing flesh, Kara almost forgot the sting.

"It's starting to swell," he murmured and kissed her one more time at the junction of thigh and shorts. Kara shivered in confused response. "We'd better get some ice on this."

He swooped her into his arms and started toward the house, coal-black eyes locked on hers in concern.

Kara buried her face against his sturdy masculine chest, hiding from the desire that still lingered. She knew he wanted her, and she wanted him. But love was out of the question, and passion wasn't enough.

Kara was frying chicken—Ty's favorite—when the backdoor clapped shut. A grimy, sweaty figure trudged into the kitchen.

"Do I know you?" Kara joked, taking in Ty's dirt-laden face, sweat-soaked shirt and filthy jeans.

Without answering, he went straight to the sink, lowered his head and turned on the cold water full force. His torso convulsed from the sudden temperature change. He was working so hard, from sunup until long after nightfall, and even though Sally and Pete kept an eye on Lane so Kara could help, the bulk of the work was on Ty. She couldn't help admire his dedication…and the way his behind looked bending over that sink.

She handed him a towel. "You're overdoing. Why don't you let some of this wait until winter?"

"Can't." He shook his head, impishly spraying her with water droplets, then stripped off his shirt and rubbed the damp towel over his glistening chest. "Those calves have to be worked soon. I'll have to hire some help with them."

"Can we afford that?" We. She'd said *we* as though they really were husband and wife working to build a life together.

Ty noticed, too, and grinned. "Kinda cool being partners, huh?"

She had to admit it was, and she felt like a drowning woman, terrified of her fate but tired of struggling against the tide of longing. She watched a single drop of water fall from Ty's hair and slither down his chest to his belly button. She swallowed hard. Quickly turning to the stove, she poked at the golden chicken, too wise and too afraid to take another chance.

The fencing pliers slipped out of Ty's gloved hand, and the entire strand of stretched barb wire catapulted toward him, wrapping around him like a bad dream. He cursed and kicked at the tangled mess, relieved to vent his frustration, considering it wasn't the only tangled mess he'd been into lately.

Kara was killing him. Plain and simple, he didn't know how much longer he could play the nice guy who wasn't the least bit bothered by her coolness. Day after day of trying to prove he was not some walk-away Joe, of trying to make her care for him again, was starting to take its toll. He had to be a complete idiot not to get the message. She was marking time until Lane was the legal heir to the ranch. Once that was done, she'd toss him out so fast he'd suffer motion sickness.

The current of sexual energy that sizzled between them was like a living thing, but Kara refused to let him love her. Was it because of Josh Riddley, the man she'd waited three years to divorce? Had she been hoping all that time that he'd come back to her? Was her claim of loathing really a cover-up? Ty was tormented with the thought that Kara wouldn't let her new husband love her because she still pined for her ex.

Maybe he'd been crazy for thinking he could be a husband in the first place. The rodeo season was in full swing. Maybe he should load up his truck and forget the whole stupid idea of settling down.

"And what would that prove, Murdock? That you're made from the same saddle blanket as your old man?"

No, by jiminy. He could pull his eight seconds on the back of a bull, and he could darn well stick out any other commitment he made. Including marriage.

With one final curse Ty swatted at a swarm of buffalo gnats and went back to the endless task of fencing. A pickup roared across the open pasture and skidded to a halt next to his. Amidst a swirl of dust, Pete and Lane slammed out the driver's side door. They were quite a pair, the old man and the kindergartner. Pete looked like a dozen other old-time ranchers in battered hat and scuffed boots. Lane resembled a greenhorn, dressed in shiny boots and creased jeans.

"Howdy, boy." Pete, thumbs in the belt loops of his baggy, faded Levi's, limped toward him. He eyed

Ty's thunderous expression and the tangled mess of wire at his feet. "A little strip of barb wire getting the best of you?"

"It's not the wire that's causing all the trouble."

"Nothing wrong with you and Kara, is there?" When Ty didn't answer, a frown formed on Pete's wrinkled brow. "Don't tell me the honeymoon's over already."

Ty rubbed a weary hand over the back of his neck. "No. I can't say that it is." How could something be over when it hadn't even begun?

"Good. Good." Relief flooded the old man's face. He leaned an elbow on the truck and shifted his weight to one side. "You gonna be working out here all morning?"

"Maybe. Why?"

By the way things were going he'd be working out here forever. A hundred acres of rotted, outdated wooden fence posts and rusty, sagging barb wire would take a while to replace.

"Ah, Sally's been fussing at me about this knee of minc." Pete lifted his hat and swiped a sleeve over his perspiring forehead. "I ain't no good to you, or me, or this place until I have it looked at, so we're fixing to head to the doc's. Kara ain't back yet to look after Lane."

With a final twist of his pliers, Ty tied off the top T-post and stood. "Where's Kara gone off to?"

"Run out of paint, she said. I told her we'd pick some up on the way back from Doc's, but you know how she is. Once she made up her mind to paint that barn, she won't stop until it's done. I figure she'll be back directly."

Studying the child's somber expression, Ty took a

red bandanna from his back pocket and swiped at the sweat on his face and neck. Judging from the rebellious look in the boy's coal-black eyes, Ty wasn't exactly number one on his list of most wanted caregivers. Hard as he'd tried, Lane was as standoffish as his mama.

"Leave the boy here. I'll look after him."

Lane shrank back, clinging to his grandfather's leg. Jiminy Christmas, he looked like he was fixing to cry. "I want to go with you, Granddad."

"Now, why do you want to go and act like that, Lane? Ty ain't gonna hurt you." Pete reached down to untwine the grasping hands. "You be a big boy, and I'll bring you that red glow-in-the-dark yo-yo you been wanting."

Lane lit up like a bonfire, releasing his iron grip on Pete's sore knee. "All right!" He punched a fist into the air and danced around in a circle, kicking up dust and aggravating the gnats.

Pete grinned and swung up into the pickup, his eyes on Ty. "Kids are simple souls. Bribery works every time."

If Ty was amazed at Lane's quick shift in mood, he was even more amazed a few minutes later. Pete's dust had barely settled around them when Lane sulled-up again. He stared after the departing truck as though it was the last lifeboat leaving the *Titanic*.

Ty studied the stiff little body, the dark, wary eyes, and a bottom lip that stuck out farther than the Texas Panhandle. What would it take to win this child?

"Mister."

"Your mama calls me Ty." He anchored one end of the wire with a well-placed boot.

"Uh-huh." Lane wandered to the fence and stared

out into the vast green pasture. "I'm gonna be a cowboy when I grow up."

"Would you like that?"

"Uh-huh. I gots to be so's I can get the ranch back."

Ty removed his gloves, holding them out to the fair-haired child. "Every cowboy has to know how to fix fence."

Lane gazed at the leather gloves, then up at Ty. His little face puckered with indecision.

"We could surprise your granddad."

His face clearing, Lane accepted the gloves. Ty stifled a smile at the tiny hands shoved into the oversize leather. He handed Lane one end of the wire.

"Walk toward that corner post with this."

Lane did as he was told, slowly unraveling the jumbled strip of metal.

"Mister?"

Ty heaved a weary sigh. They lived in the same house, and Lane still called him mister. "What?"

"Where's all the horses?"

"Out there somewhere," Ty indicated with a sweep of one hand.

"A cowboy gots to have a horse, don't he? You gots a real pretty horse. Mama gots Taffy."

"Yep." Ty gazed down the fence row at the little figure in boots and hat. He was backpeddling, expression wistful, talking all the while about horses. What was the boy getting at?

Suddenly, the answer jolted him like a whiplash. Lane wanted his own horse. A grin broke across his face. Maybe old Pete was right about kids and bribery.

* * *

"Mama! Mama!"

Seat belt stretched to the limit, Lane hung out the window of Ty's pickup, yelling at the top of his lungs.

Kara, whose neck and shoulders ached from the constant up-and-down motion of painting, paused and shaded her eyes against the glare bouncing off Ty's big silver and blue truck. Horse trailer in tow, it rumbled to a stop outside the paddock.

"Hurry, Mom, hurry. Come see."

Propping the paintbrush atop the can, Kara grabbed a turpentine rag and started toward her son, wiping red paint from her hands as she went.

"Dad said you two were out building fence."

Ty, who'd hopped out the driver's side door, reached back for Lane, swinging him onto the grass. "We had more important things to do, didn't we, partner?"

The pair looked at Kara, identical grins creasing their tanned faces. Her breath caught, and her heart thudded with an odd mix of pleasure and pain. Side by side, both dressed in cowboy gear, they looked so handsome and so much alike. How long would it be before someone else commented on that likeness?

Lane grabbed her hand, tugging her toward the trailer, his excitement palpable. "Come see, Mama. He's a real beaut. That's what Ty says."

In the face of her son's excitement, Kara shoved her worries aside and glanced toward her temporary husband, acknowledging the little buzz of excitement that zipped through her veins every time she saw him. "What have you done, Murdock?"

Grabbing her other hand, he repeated Lane's plea, his own eagerness as evident as that of the child. "Come see."

Kara knew she shouldn't let him touch her. His warm calloused palm felt way too good against her own. Too often lately her daytime thoughts and night-time dreams were more and more of Ty as her husband for real. It was a dangerous game, a tightrope between what felt so good and what she knew to be right. Still, she left her hand in his.

A soft equine whicker sounded from inside the trailer. The animal's snow-white tail and golden rump showed above the gate.

"He's a panamilo, Mama. Ain't he a beaut?"

"Isn't he," she corrected, smiling at her son's exuberant mispronunciation of palomino.

"He sure is. Ty says he's gentle as a dog, and he's all mine."

"He said that, did he?" Her gaze went from Lane to Ty, who looked as boyishly delighted as her son.

"You don't mind, do you?" Ty asked.

"Nothing could please me more."

His black eyes locked on her green ones. "Nothing?"

Kara's heart set up a drumbeat. She knew that look. Those sparkling eyes, that sexy grin were getting harder to resist.

"Ty," she warned, "don't start it today."

"Why not?" Ty's mouth quirked with humor. "You are my wife."

"Not really." Was that regret or caution?

He inched closer, bringing the scent of sweat and sun and something undeniably male. Her entire body went on red alert, straining toward him with every fiber. "It doesn't have to be that way."

She swallowed—hard. "Yes, it does."

Ty's voice softened. Lightly he traced her set jaw with one finger. "Give me one good reason."

Goose bumps prickled beneath his touch. Kara's breath grew suddenly shallow.

She could give him a dozen reasons, but the most important one stood three feet away, oblivious to the current running between the two adults. After years of protecting her son, her father and her own broken heart, she couldn't give in to physical attraction. That's all it was, this dementia she experienced every time he touched her.

Kara pulled away, though the warmth of Ty's touch and the pull of his personality lingered. A curious throb of loss pulsed in her veins. She reached inside the trailer and patted the new horse, grateful for the neutral ground of horse and child.

Apparently, since she'd seen them last, Lane's estimation of the new man in his life had increased significantly. She'd never even seen him smile at Ty. Now, hero worship suffused his upturned face.

"Get him out, Ty." Lane hopped up and down. "I want to ride him."

Ty hesitated. "I don't know, bud—"

Kara knelt in front of her son, grasping his chin. "Lane, baby, we can't ride your horse today."

"Why not? He's mine. Ty said so. I want to ride 'im."

"He needs a day or two to get used to his new home. He's probably a little nervous right now."

"Oh." Dejection settled over the child like a dust cloud.

"Hey, partner," Ty hunkered down beside Kara, his shoulder brushing hers. When she skittered away, he gave her a slow appraisal and a knowing, impudent wink. Then he turned his attention to Lane. "How about a ride on Cochise?"

Lane brightened. "Really?"

"Your mama can saddle up Taffy and come, too. Right, Kara?"

It was her turn to hesitate. His gift to their son had stirred all kinds of warm, fuzzy yearnings. And lately she was having a much harder time recalling the heartache of the past. Was this the kind of woman she'd become? Like Jolene, Ty's sister, was she a sucker for a few kind words and a moment of passion?

"I don't think so..." Newly wary of her ability to make the right decision, she shook her head.

"Please, Mama, please." Lane started bouncing again, his joy fully returned at the promise of a horseback ride with the two adults.

Ty's black eyes twinkled. "Come on, Kara," he coaxed. "What can it hurt?"

Dang him, he knew she was softening.

"That barn won't paint itself."

"It'll still be here tomorrow."

"Please, Mama, please."

With an exasperated sigh Kara caved in. "Oh, all right."

Though the sun was hot, a breeze kicked up as the trio aimed their horses across open pasture. Lane, perched on the saddle in front of Ty, proudly held the reins. Ty rested one arm at his side while the other twined around the child's waist, ready to handle the horse if the need arose. Cochise, usually a spirited mount, ambled quietly beside the more sedate Taffy.

"It's pretty warm out here. You two want to stop at the creek and rest a bit?"

"No." Kara's quick answer brought a smirk to Ty's dark face. The last place she wanted to go was that danged creek, and he knew it. Memories of long-ago summers, of youthful passion, of making impossible wishes on faraway stars tumbled back every time she thought of that shady nook beside the flowing water.

"Scaredy-cat," Ty taunted, grinning at her across the top of Lane's white hat.

She shrugged, feigning indifference. "If you want to ride to the creek, it's fine with me."

Ty, the ornery cuss, headed straight toward their favorite spot, dismounted and collapsed with a contented sigh on the shady bank.

"I love this place. Don't you, Kara?"

Kara, who stood several feet from the reclining males, focused her attention on the cool, clear water rippling over the rocky bottom. Anything to quiet the aching memories.

"We used to go skinny-dipping when it was hot like this." Ty's lazy, teasing words were directed at Lane, but Kara knew they were meant to get a rise out of her. She glared at him, hoping he'd have sense enough not to say too much in front of a child.

Lane screwed up his face, squinting with curiosity and admiration at the cowboy he'd despised only a few hours earlier. "What's skinny-dipping?"

With a chuckle Ty said, "Stripping down to your drawers to go swimming."

"You and Mama did that?" Lane's eyes grew round and curious.

"Ty!" Kara admonished as she moved over to squat down beside her son. "Not together, sweetie. And it was long, long ago when we very little kids."

She dared that maniac to contradict her.

"Little like me?" The child was all trust and innocence which made telling a white lie all the harder for his mother.

"Well…yes. Pretty little."

"Can I go skimpy-dipping?" Lane looked hopefully at the cool, clear stream.

"No!"

"Ah, why not, Kara? It's hot, and we're right here to watch him. Strip him down to his shorts, and let him play."

"Stay out of this, Murdock. You've done quite enough as it is."

"Please, Mama?" Lane was already tugging at his boots.

"Skinny-dipping is a fine American tradition." Ty tossed a twig in her direction. "All *little kids* should do it."

One glance at Ty's amused face told her he remembered two very big kids, heated by more than the Texas sun, cavorting in the water. Surely he wouldn't say so in front of a five-year-old child, but with Murdock she dared not take the chance.

Kara threw her hands up and surrendered. Lane was already down to his briefs, heading toward the creek.

"Stay close to the bank," Kara called in a last ditch effort to reestablish her parental authority. Neither Murdock nor Lane appeared the least impressed. "Those rocks get mossy and slick."

Bright sun glistened on the water, though the bank was shaded by an arc of trees. After a few tentative toe touches and a squeal of delight, Lane plunged into the creek. Water rose to his thighs. Kara and Ty settled on the bank. Ty stretched out, propped on one elbow. Kara sat several feet away, hugging her upraised knees, attention riveted on her son.

"You've done a fine job with him, Kara," Ty said, surprising her. "He's a good kid. Smart as a whip."

"Thank you."

"It couldn't have been easy. After the divorce, I mean."

"We managed."

"I'd have helped, you know, even though he's someone else's son. I owed you that much."

She stiffened. Talking about this was dangerous. "All you owe me is this ranch."

"I'm working on that."

She shifted her head in his direction, eyebrows arched questioningly.

"Old Culpepper started the adoption proceedings last week." Ty yanked a grass stem and studied it. "I've already signed papers that will make Lane my heir as soon as the adoption goes through."

"You never cease to amaze me, Murdock."

"I'm a pretty amazing guy, all right."

"Modest, too."

Tickling her leg with a stem of grass, Ty smiled— not the devil-may-care grin he usually wore, but a soft, wistful thing that stroked Kara's insides in much the same way the grass stroked her thigh.

"We could make this work if we set our minds to it."

She didn't pretend not to understand his meaning. Deep in her soul she wished he was right, but there were too many complications and she was too afraid to trust herself again. "I don't think so."

"What changed you, Kara? What caused you to build a wall so high around yourself and Lane that no one can get inside?" His voice was low, mesmerizing. "Was it your marriage? Was it me?"

"Ty, don't..." Kara brushed away the tickling grass. Ty dropped his hand and sat up, scooting closer to her—way too close. Her skin tingled in that peculiar way it had whenever he brushed against her. He made things worse by sliding an arm across her shoulders.

"We could do it, Kara." His warm breath nuzzled her ear. "We could."

Was it possible? With all the baggage in their backgrounds, could they really make their marriage work? Could she really let go and believe in him—in herself?

"Do you know why I wanted to marry you?" he surprised her by asking.

"I have to admit that's puzzled me some. You could have made Lane your heir without a marriage license."

"I didn't marry you to make someone else's son my heir."

She stiffened, his words reminding her of the unbreachable chasm between them. "That was your idea."

"Now, don't get huffy. This place should belong to Lane. I got no problem with that. I'm just telling you that he wasn't the reason I married you. And the ranch wasn't the reason I married you." He nuzzled her ear, his voice dropping to a husky whisper. "*You're* the reason I married you."

Was he trying to say he loved her? That he regretted their parting? That he longed to erase the wrong he'd done to her? The iceberg lodged inside Kara's heart for so long began to melt. She wanted to believe. She desperately wanted to believe.

At that moment she acknowledged what she'd fought from the beginning. She still loved him. Fool that she was, she loved the rambling cowboy, Ty Murdock.

A wind whispered in the trees above them, and sunlight speckled the patch of thick clover beneath them. Memories of stretching out on that clover, with Ty following her down, kissing, teasing, loving, rolled through her mind.

He'd been her hero, her lover, her friend. When her mother died, Ty was the one to comfort her, holding her while she wept and wailed and screamed at life's injustice. He stood between her and Pete at the funeral, stoically holding them both together, though his own eyes were suspiciously red the whole time. She'd once been so secure in his love.

Sadness quivered through her. She'd trusted him, and he'd let her down. Could she ever believe in him again? Was it really possible to go back? She was so terribly, terribly afraid.

A tiny muscle twitched below one of Ty's onyx eyes. His gaze fell to her mouth, stayed there.

He was going to kiss her, and she wanted it badly. Not the wild lust they'd shared in the barnyard, but a kiss of love. Just for one moment she wanted to believe in happy endings.

"Kara?" He sounded insecure, worried. Was he as frightened by this as she?

Her blood began to hum, the special music that played only for Ty Murdock. She felt herself giving in, forgetting, longing to trust and love again.

He kissed her then. Softly, tentatively as though he'd never done it before. Carefully testing the waters in a way so endearingly unlike Ty Murdock that Kara completely capitulated. With a sigh of surrender she wrapped both arms around him and returned the kiss.

When the kiss ended, Kara pulled away, confused, flooded by a torrent of emotion. Would Ty want her if he knew about Lane? Or would he feel betrayed and renege on his promise to give Lane the ranch? As much as she longed to tell him the truth, she wasn't ready to trust him with her most precious secret.

"I don't think this is such a good idea, Murdock," she murmured through lips that ached to be kissed again.

He studied her for a long, serious moment, then shifted away. Kara knew she'd hurt him, and the knowledge both surprised and pained her.

"I'm sorry," she started.

"Hey, no hard feelings." He gave a short, self-deprecating laugh. "Well, some of my feelings might be a little hard, but none that I won't get over in a few minutes."

His defenses were back, sheathed in flippancy. But this time she knew and was truly sorry for all the wounds that couldn't heal.

"Ty." Intending a truce, she gently laid a palm against the angle of his jaw. What she felt there changed the direction of her thinking. "Murdock, you're hot."

"That's what all the ladies say."

"No, I'm serious." She touched his forehead. "I think you have a fever."

"I do feel kinda funny."

That, at least, explained his mellow mood.

"What kind of funny?"

"I don't know. My skin's kind of crawly." He looked around the clover. "You don't suppose we're sitting on ants, do you?"

Kara clapped a hand to her mouth, stifling the giggle that threatened. "Unbutton your shirt."

"Now you're talking!" He ripped the snaps in one fluid motion. "Are we going skinny-dipping, too?"

"We are not going skinny-dipping. I'm checking your back for chicken pox. That's where they start."

"No!" He slithered out of her reach, struggling to replace his shirt.

"Stop being a baby. If you have them, you have them."

"But you'll enjoy it so much if I do," he moaned, clearly aghast.

"Yes, I will." She slapped away his resisting hands. "Now, let me look."

To her utter disappointment his back was as smooth and clear as polished oak.

"Shoot. No pox." With a sigh Kara flopped onto the grass.

Ty wore a ridiculously injured expression. "Couldn't chicken pox have made me—" he gazed down at his zipper and shuddered "—you know, sterile?"

She didn't dare answer that one, not with her lips still tingling from his kiss and her body still craving his touch.

Ty shivered against the soft breeze, and gooseflesh dimpled his skin. Sitting up, Kara looked into his glassy black eyes and pressed a hand to his forehead. He was definitely coming down with something. Must be the fever making his skin crawly.

"Kara. Hey." He pushed her hand away. "Enough."

"Oh, Murdock, you're such a bad sport."

"Sure I am. But that's not important right now. It's Lane."

Sobering, Kara turned, searching the creek for her son. How could she have let her attention wander that way?

"He's getting too far away from us. We'd better stop him."

Lane was at least a hundred yards downstream where the creek took a sharp plunge into a deep canyon.

"Lane, come back this way," she called.

"Ah, Mama." Lane took several more steps, ignoring his mother's command.

"Get back up here this minute, young man."

With a disgusted heave of his entire body, the child flopped around and started upstream. Mutinous, he dragged his feet and plodded along, kicking at rocks and splashing water.

Fifty yards out he lost his footing and slipped, facedown, into the creek.

"Lane!" Kara shrieked. Springing up from the ground, she started toward the water. "He's not getting up!"

Using the quick reflexes that made him a champion rider, Ty darted past her, hit the water running and never slowed down until he reached the fallen child. Whitecaps of churned water spewed around his boot-clad feet as he yanked Lane up with one quick grab.

Blood covered the child's mouth and nose. Hoisting him easily, Ty carried Lane to the bank and placed him in Kara's trembling arms.

Wide-eyed and crying, Lane's wet body shivered against his mother. Blood smeared her shirtfront.

"Where is all that blood coming from?" Kara, who

considered herself panic proof, felt the fraying edges of hysteria taking control. "Is his nose broken? All his teeth gone? What is it?"

Ty grabbed his discarded shirt from the grass and patted gently at Lane's face. "I don't see anything on the outside. Open your mouth, partner. Let me look inside."

Obediently, the sniffling child opened his mouth. Both rows of tiny white teeth were intact.

"He bit his tongue."

"That's all? Just his tongue?" Kara trembled with relief.

"Yep. A little ice or a Popsicle will fix him right up." Ty stretched his arms toward the child. "Let me have him before you fall down."

"I don't usually get this upset."

"It was a scary moment."

Kara loved him for saying that, for not poking fun at her emotional reaction. In all the excitement Ty's illness had completely slipped her mind. Belatedly she told him, "You shouldn't get chilled."

Pulling the wet boy close, he gave a little shiver. "This heat will dry me out. Grab his clothes, and let's head home."

"You've ruined your shirt." She indicated the expensive white cotton snugged against Lane's protruding tongue.

"It's nothing." He carried Lane to the horse. "Can you ride, little partner?"

"Yeth."

"That a boy. You're a brave cowboy, you know it?"

Kara shoved jeans and a T-shirt toward her son and mounted Taffy. Ty gently slipped the T-shirt over

Lane's head and draped the jeans across his knees. With the strong dark hands that could handle a bull or a bucking horse, Ty tenderly pulled the boy into a protective embrace.

Kara's heart hurt to watch. Ty Murdock, for all his faults, would be a wonderful father to his son.

Chapter Nine

"Thirteen," Ty muttered.

"What?" Kara stopped polishing the old mahogany dresser and glanced over one shoulder. What she saw brought a grin to her lips. Propped up in bed, the all-round champion carefully counted out thirteen pennies. Next to him, Lane sat cross-legged, a triumphant expression on his adorable face.

"This little sodbuster's won thirteen of my hard-earned pennies." Ty slapped a hand against his thigh in mock dismay. Kara's eyes nearly crossed looking at the ripple of that dark corded muscle. "Thirteen. That has to be unlucky. Might cause me to take another chill."

Suffering from a rapidly disappearing case of summer flu, Ty was naked except for a pair of boxer shorts bedecked with longhorn skulls. Clothes, he claimed, made him hot.

Flu or not, his dark, nude body made Kara hot. Tending his exaggerated state of illness had stretched her willpower to the limits. When she'd protested his state of undress, Ty had only wiggled his eyebrows and reminded her that they were, after all, married and that she was welcome to join him in the big ol' bed anytime she took a mind to. The only thing that kept her sane—and out of that big ol' bed—was bantering, giving him tit for tat.

"If you're real unlucky you'll get a fever blister on the end of your…" She raised an eyebrow, letting him finish the suggestion with his imagination.

"Why, Kara Dean, I'm shocked." He grinned wickedly, clearly not shocked at all.

She tossed a towel at him. "I was gonna say nose."

"And ruin this pretty face of mine?" Ty cast a glance of feigned horror toward Lane. "Your mama has a mean streak, you know that?"

"She took real good care of me when I had the chicken pops." Holding a deck of cards while he raked his pennies into a pile, Lane paid little attention to the curious byplay between the two adults. He'd clearly decided Ty was a hero worthy of his attention. "You want to play 'Go Fish' again?"

Heaving an exaggerated sigh, Ty nodded. "Why not? We can't go out and play. Nurse Ratchet won't let us."

"Tomorrow will be soon enough." Kara spurted one last shot of Murphy's Oil Soap on the dresser and wiped it dry. "We can't have you collapsing in this heat after such a *life threatening* illness."

Ty laughed, his teeth gleaming against dark skin. He'd played his fever to the hilt, letting her pamper him. All the while, his dark, suggestive gaze followed her around the room, burning holes in her carefully erected wall of protection.

"Don't worry, Ty. You'll get better soon." Lane, bless his heart, had set up camp in Ty's room, doing his best to entertain his new buddy.

"He *is* better," Kara insisted. "Anyone this restless has to be on the mend. If he was really sick, he'd just lie there like week-old road kill."

Lane giggled. Ty groaned.

"Vicious. She's vicious, I tell you."

Lane giggled again. "Yeah, but I love her. Don't you?"

Over his cards the accursed cowboy shot her a wicked look and winked. "I sure do, little partner."

Even though he was joking, a jolt of happiness hummed through her veins. Ever since the day at the creek when she'd watched him ride home with Lane cradled against his chest, heedless of his own feverish body, she'd been helpless to stop thinking of him. He'd put his son's welfare before his own and then paid dearly for it by having a miserable episode of chills. And his work around the ranch showed nothing if not complete dedication to his new home. He truly seemed determined to settle down and leave the rodeo behind.

Had Ty really changed? Had he meant it when he'd said they could make it? Was it really possible to wipe away the hurt and anger that had lingered for so very long? She loved him, but could she trust him? Could she trust herself to decide?

She wanted to. Yet she couldn't forget how she'd given him everything, only to have him leave her alone and pregnant while he cavorted with Shannon Sullivan.

But he didn't know about the baby, a little voice in

her head nagged. Would things have been different if he had?

The question was unanswerable. They'd both done what they'd done, and there was no going back.

Cleaner and rag beneath one arm, Kara yanked the soiled sheets from the end of the bed and started out of the room. She'd had all of his nude body she could take for one morning. "You two entertain each other. I want to get this place cleaned while you're out of my hair."

Ty's head popped up from his perusal of the brightly colored cards. "No need to bother with the office. I'll clean that myself. Too much junk in there for you to worry with."

Something in his tone, and the way he avoided her eyes, gave Kara pause. She stared at him questioningly for two beats before turning on her heel. What was Murdock hiding?

Ty let Lane beat him at two more games of "Go Fish" before it occurred to him that he didn't want to play sick anymore. Since the original episode of chills three days ago, he'd actually felt fine. But he *had* relished Kara's attention, the way her hands felt on his skin, the way she looked and smelled so sweet, the way her round little behind and smooth, tanned thighs looked in a pair of shorts. Jiminy! If he hadn't had a fever, she'd have given him one. She was driving him wild with need, and he couldn't take another minute of it. An outdoor kind of a guy couldn't lie around in bed forever—unless he had company, of course. He cast a rueful glance at Lane. The boy wasn't exactly the company he had in mind.

"Little partner, what's say we blow this joint?"

"Huh?" Lane's dark brows knit together in confusion.

"Let's sneak out to the barn and check on that pony of yours," Ty said in a conspiratorial whisper.

Lane looked doubtful, but he slipped the cards into their holder and crawled off the bed. "Mama might get mad."

"That's why we're going to be very, very quiet." Going to the closet, Ty pulled out jeans and a shirt and tossed them on the bed. He'd just started to dress when Kara appeared in the doorway.

"What are you doing?"

"Oops, busted." He cast a sideways grimace at Lane, then turned his attention to Kara. She looked funny. Her cheeks were red, her eyes glassy as if she had a fever. His tomfoolery disappeared. "Are you getting sick, too?"

"I'm sick, all right. Sick of being lied to." She pulled a stack of envelopes from behind her back, her hand trembling. "What are these?"

She wasn't sick. She was furious. Ty dropped the shirt he held. "I told you to stay out of the office."

"What I don't know won't hurt me. Is that what you think?"

"It's just a few bills, Kara." Bills he'd intended to pay the day he'd gotten sick. Bills he hadn't expected, hadn't been prepared for.

"I looked at the ledgers." Kara spoke between gritted teeth, clearly losing the battle to keep her temper. "You've got this ranch into such bad financial shape, we may lose it."

Ty dragged a hand over his face and let out a slow, weary breath. How did he get out of this one without breaking his promise to Pete?

"Look, Kara, I'm taking care of it, okay? It's not your concern."

With a temper like hers, he should have known she wouldn't hold back long. She exploded like an atom bomb. "None of my concern? This is my son's life! I won't stand by and watch you destroy everything my father worked for."

Ty was starting to tire of the villain role. His own voice rose several decibels. "Leave it alone, Kara."

"I will not leave it alone." Hands fisted, face flaming, she stormed across the room. "My poor trusting father. He cares about you. How could you do this to him?"

They were both at full volume now.

"I care more about your father than you'll ever know."

"He's spent his whole life building this place." Trembling, she met him nose to nose and yelled. "Seeing this ranch sink in a sea of debt will kill him."

Before he could stop himself, Ty shouted into her contorted face. "They're his bills."

Kara stumbled back, the steam seeping out of her. "My daddy would never let bills pileup like this," she countered in disbelief.

"Face it, Kara. Nobody is perfect. You make mistakes. He makes mistakes. Hell, I've made mistakes. If you weren't so all-fired determined to keep that Taylor pride intact, you could see that your dad couldn't keep up with this place anymore. Things just got away from him. He needed help."

"And you're trying to tell me you were that help? That you took over my ranch out of the goodness of your heart?"

"Yes!" Ty gripped her shoulders, wanting to make

her see the truth. Wanting her to stop expecting the worst from him. He wasn't his daddy, couldn't she see that?

The two adults were so intent on their own raging emotions that they'd forgotten the boy standing next to the bed. But when Ty put his hands on Kara, Lane erupted in a wild flurry of arms and legs.

"Leave my Mama alone!" he cried, kicking and punching with all his five-year-old strength. "Don't you hit her! Don't you hit her!"

Both adults froze. Kara paled and fell to her knees beside the thrashing child. She gripped his arms. "Stop it, Lane. Stop it right now. Ty isn't going to hit me."

"That's right, little man." All anger forgotten in the face of the child's fright, Ty pulled Lane into his arms. "A cowboy doesn't hit his woman. He takes care of her."

"My dad hit her."

At Kara's sharp intake of breath, Ty raised his gaze to hers and read the truth there.

He'd been stomped once by a bull. The hoof caught him square in the gut just as he landed on the soft arena floor. All the air went from him. He'd gasped and struggled for precious oxygen, but breath hadn't returned for the longest time. He felt that way now.

They knelt there on the floor, silent and stunned, the horror of the boy's words pulsating between them. A combination of rage, pain and guilt slammed through Ty. He had to know what had happened—and why she'd allowed it. But not with the boy listening wide-eyed and afraid.

Ty balanced the shaking child on one knee. "Lane." He tilted the child's chin upward. Black, worried eyes studied him. "Your mom and I need to talk about some things. Why don't you go over to Granddad's for a awhile?"

Lane looked doubtful. "Are you gonna yell some more?"

"You have my word of honor as a cowboy." Gently he stroked the thick blond hair. "I'm not gonna yell."

"You won't hit her, will you?"

Ty groaned and kissed the boy's forehead. The question was like a knife in the gut. "I promise never to hit your mama."

The child's trembling eased.

Kara stirred. "It's okay, baby. Ty would never, ever hurt either one of us." Pale and trembling, she hugged him and put her lips where Ty's had been a moment before. "Tell Granddad we have some talking to do, and we'll come get you later."

Kara moved to the telephone beside the bed and called Pete to let him know Lane was on his way. She replaced the receiver but remained where she was, staring at the white, textured wall.

Swallowing past the knot in his throat, Ty grasped her arm and pulled her around as gently as he knew how.

"Your husband hit you?" he asked quietly.

Her eyes grew round and wet. Her lips turned down, quivering. "Lane was so little. I thought he was too young to remember." Tears gathered, overflowed and slithered down her cheeks. "I didn't want him to remember."

"Oh, Kara. I'm sorry. So very sorry." Unable to restrain the flood of emotion inside him, Ty drew her fiercely against his naked chest. Guilt and remorse ripped at him. "If I hadn't been such a fool... If I hadn't left you alone..."

Kara's tears wet his skin, and he thought his heart would explode. The only woman he'd ever loved had suffered at the hands of an abuser because of him. How could he live with knowing he'd failed her so completely. No wonder she was afraid to let him love her. He was as selfish and undependable as his father.

"Did you love him? Is that why you put up with it?"

"No. No." Voice adamant, she shook her head. "I never loved him. Never."

"Then, why?"

"Lane," she admitted, in a tortured whisper. "I married him because of Lane."

The admission confirmed his fear—that she'd been pregnant when she married Josh Riddley. The truth hurt as much as he'd expected. On the rebound from him, because of his leaving her, Kara had sought comfort from the first man who'd offered it.

"I'd never have left you with a man like that." He bracketed her small face in his hands and kissed the streaming tears. "Why didn't you wait for me?"

She blanched and tried to pull away, but Ty gripped her shoulders and drew her to him.

"Why?" he demanded.

"Shannon Sullivan," she admitted, voice breaking.

"Shannon Sullivan?" He blinked in confusion. "What did she have to do with you and me?"

"You know what the two of you did." Kara bit her bottom lip and thrust her chin upward. Her nose was red and her eyes damp with tears, but the Taylor pride exerted itself. "Less than a month after you left, I ran into her. She couldn't wait to tell me about your cozy little setup." Fresh tears puddled on her eyelids.

A frown gathered between Ty's eyebrows. He had a vague memory of dancing with the overblown blonde who hung out in all the favorite rodeo haunts and went home with whichever cowboy asked her. "There was never anything between Shannon and me."

Kara shook her head in disbelief; tears started afresh. Though she dashed at them with the back of her hand, they flowed on. "She was after you all through high school, hating me because I was in the way. Once you were on the road, she made her move. She told me so."

Kara tried to pull away, but Ty held fast. He had to make her understand. With all the sincerity in him, he gazed into her wounded green eyes.

"She lied, Kara. Shannon was one of the groupies that hung around the rodeos, but she was any cowboy's woman."

"She wanted you."

"I was building a rodeo career, not chasing women. Why won't you believe that?" He clenched his teeth. "I am not my father. I never cheated on you with Shannon Sullivan. Never!"

Kara's body went slack. Horror and regret swept her face.

"You mean—" her voice fell to a whimper "—I didn't have to marry Josh?"

What was left of his heart flew right out of his chest. She'd suffered so much.

"Ah, baby. How can I make it up to you?" With fierce tenderness, his lips traveled over her face, her eyes, her cheeks. "Let me make it up to you."

Aching with the need to heal all her wounds in the only way he knew how, Ty's hungry, desperate mouth found hers. When, with a whimper of surrender Kara pressed into him, Ty lost whatever thought he'd had of gently rekindling their love. Every cell in his body cried out for this woman who was his heart and soul. His blood pumped wildly. The weeks of denial built to a crescendo.

Kara responded in kind, her satin hands stroking his naked back and chest, moving over him until he thought his knees would buckle. Her soft mewling sounds shook him to the core. A deep groan erupted from his lips as he walked her backward toward the bed.

"I never stopped wanting you," he rasped against her throat. "You and nobody else."

He'd waited so long for this moment, for Kara to accept him again. Just as her knees bumped the mattress, Ty pulled away and stared into her flushed face. He wanted her to know—she had to understand—that he would never have intentionally stayed away while another man hurt her. "I would have come back if I'd known about your baby."

The change in Kara was instantaneous. She froze as if doused with ice water. Though her heart still hammered against his, she no longer responded to his kisses. Her breath came in short gasps, her eyes wide with some emotion other than passion. Pushing at his chest, she broke contact with his thrumming body.

"Kara?" What had he done wrong? What had he said? He racked his brain but nothing came. He'd been so caught up in the joy of having her in his arms again that he had no idea what she was upset about. He reached for her again, but she stepped away.

"I shouldn't have done that." She thrust out her chin. The unshed tears trembling on her lashes nearly broke him in two.

Before he could protest, she rushed out of the bedroom, leaving her sweet taste and feel imprinted on his body. While he stood stunned and bewildered, he heard the backdoor close.

What was going on? One minute she responded like a woman in love and the next she ran out on him. Were his kisses that lousy? Had he come on too strong?

He slapped his forehead as the idea struck. She'd just confessed how Riddley had taken her love and then abused her, and what had he done in response? He'd grabbed at her like a sex starved maniac.

"You're losing it, Murdock," he mumbled, shaking his head. "The woman needs tenderness and romancing, but all you can think of is jumping her bones."

He kicked the bedpost. Pain shot up his foot. He hopped around holding his big toe, perversely glad for the punishment. He'd let her down. Again. Try as he might, his father's genes kept popping out of him like cold sores.

Chapter Ten

"Are you busy?"

Kara gasped and whirled around, hairbrush in hand. "Ty! I didn't hear you come in."

He was freshly showered, his hair damp and glossy. Even after a long day on the troubled ranch, he managed to look incredible.

Heat crept into her face. Ever since yesterday's fiasco she'd avoided him, and now here he was, standing in her bedroom. She hadn't known what to say, how to explain her odd behavior. One minute she was all over him, practically begging for his love and the next she was tortured with the realization that he'd never cheated her. She'd cheated him. If he ever found out, who knew what he might do? He could take her family's ranch, and with adoption procedures underway, maybe even her child. But most important, he'd be devastated, and the desire and tenderness she saw on his face would turn to hatred.

Ty eyed the turned-back bed, the nightgown lying across its foot. "You tired?"

Just having him look at her nighty started wild images swirling in her head. Kara swallowed past the guilt and tension and forced a civil reply.

"Not really." Turning away, she reached for a green scrunchie. When her hand trembled, she let it drop, leaving her hair down. "With Lane over at Dad's for the night, I didn't bother to cook. If you're hungry I can fix you something."

"I have a surprise." He stretched a hand toward her. "Come see."

"I don't think that's a good idea."

"Ah, come on, Kara. Can't we enjoy each other's company? See where it takes us? I won't force anything. I promise."

She averted her eyes as he inadvertently drove the stab of guilt deeper. "I know all your tricks, Murdock."

With one finger he lifted her chin, his twinkling eyes wicked. "Maybe I've learned some new ones."

In spite of herself she smiled. "I don't doubt that."

"Then, come on. Take a chance. See what I'm up to." A smile tipped the corners of his mouth, teasing and serious at the same time. "What can it hurt?"

What *could* it hurt? Things couldn't get much worse.

"You're certainly mysterious tonight." But she slipped her feet into a pair of sandals and followed him out the door and to the barn. Two saddled horses awaited them.

"Are we going somewhere?"

"Yep."

"But you're not telling me where?"

"Nope." He held a red cloth out to her. "I want you to wear this."

"A bandanna?"

"A blindfold."

Electric quivers of delight danced over her skin, leaving gooseflesh in their wake. She drew away. "Let you blindfold me? You're dreaming again, Murdock."

"Scared?"

"No!" Then, "Maybe. What *are* you up to?" The idea of riding blindfold with Ty was both titillating and terrifying.

He held out the bandanna. "Only one way to find out."

She knew it was unwise, given the terrible secret between them, but Kara couldn't resist the temptation to see where this was leading. Every nerve ending vibrated as he turned her around to cover her eyes with the bandanna. Lifting her hair from her neck, he skimmed his lips over the nape, and laughed huskily when she shivered and skittered sideways. His strong hands lifted her into the saddle.

Tugging at her dress, she adjusted it beneath her, leaving more leg exposed than she liked. She jumped when Ty smoothed a hand from her thigh to her ankle. The touch of his skin warmed her long after he stepped away.

With practiced ease, Cochise and Taffy carried their riders across the wide meadow. After another hot day the night had cooled. Crickets and tree frogs trilled in chorus. Somewhere deep in the woods, a bobwhite quail whistled his name, and way in the distance a coyote called to his mate.

Without benefit of vision, the smells and sounds of the summer night intensified around her.

"Something's blooming down here." Ty's hushed words raised new goose bumps on Kara's arms.

"Honeysuckle. Smells good." Her own voice sounded husky.

The soft, plodding rhythm of hoofbeats against thick grass, the snuffle of equine breathing, the occasional creak of leather or jingle of tack wove a magic spell. Ty didn't touch her again, but she could feel him there beside her. The sweet electricity pulsing between them spoke volumes.

Long before they reached their destination, Kara smelled the water, felt its coolness on her skin. When the horses stopped, Ty lifted her to the ground and pulled her close. With her blindfold still in place, he bracketed her face, raised it to his. Though her mind clearly demanded she stop this nonsense, her heart wouldn't obey. When Ty kissed her with exquisite tenderness, Kara wanted to forget all the pain between them and go with the emotion.

Her heart thudded as he swept her into his arms. "Ty?"

"Shh." His breath was warm against her cheek.

Arms around his warm, soap-scented neck, she heard the babble of water, the croak and plop of startled frogs, and felt the gentle jarring of rough terrain.

When she was tenderly lowered to a standing position, she again waited. It was crazy. It was irrational, but she had never felt such exquisite humming in her blood.

Behind her, his hands on the blindfold, Ty's low voice caressed her ear. "Ready?"

With a delicious shiver, she nodded.

"Close your eyes."

Pulse pounding, her belly whirling in anticipation,

she obeyed, too intrigued and turned-on to do anything else. What was this crazy cowboy up to?

The bandanna slipped off, and Ty moved away. She strained toward the sounds, intrigued, excited.

She heard a scratching, then smelled a faint sulfur-scent of smoke that disappeared almost as quickly as it came. A hint of roses hung in the air.

"Don't jump, and don't look." Ty's whispery, mysterious tone was seductive.

Something popped loudly, and she was glad for his warning. There was a tinkling, a splash, a rustle, and then silence.

"Okay," he murmured from somewhere in front of her. "Open your eyes."

The sight sent her heart rate from wild to insane. She wasn't sure what she'd been expecting, a new colt perhaps, but certainly not this. He'd brought her to the clearing along the creek bank where the trees formed a semicircle, shutting out the rest of the world. A patchwork quilt, covered with fresh rose petals, was spread over the thick clover bed, a silver champagne bucket in its center. Beside it, a picnic basket held two crystal plates on its top. To either side, candlelight flickered white and shimmering from two tall tapers.

Ty knelt before the glimmering candles, a fluted glass in each hand, looking his sexiest. His dark, crisp hair glistened clean and damp in the candlelight. His onyx eyes sparkled with mischief. His shirt was opened all the way, revealing the washboard belly and strong chest that Kara adored. With a quirk of one eyebrow, he extended a glass toward her.

"Join me, Mrs. Murdock?"

Mrs. Murdock. He'd never called her that, and the

notion turned her insides to mush. What was he doing? What did this mean?

Trembling, touched to the soul, she went, kneeling on the rose petals opposite him. The sweet fragrance wafted up, wrapping them both in its beauty. Kara took the offered glass and sipped once, watching her husband over the rim.

"Like it?" He sounded anxious.

"Why? I don't understand."

"Because I want to. To make up for all the hurt."

So that was it. He felt sorry for her. Would he feel the same if she told him? A little of her excitement vanished. "I want to forget the past, Murdock."

"Can you?"

"Yes," she lied. It was almost the truth. She could forget about Josh, forget his abuse. She could even forget how badly Ty had hurt her when he left. But she could never forget the secret that stood between them.

"Open."

A chocolate-covered strawberry came her way. "No." She shook her head, but Ty wouldn't be denied. He pressed the sweet fruit against her lips until she opened.

She'd been alone so long, and every day she found more about him to love. Did she dare go with the exquisite feeling between them?

Gesturing toward the basket, she teased, "Don't you have any fried chicken in there?"

"Nope. Just sexy food. Strawberries, wine." He waggled both eyebrows and reached into the basket. "Even have some whipped cream in here."

Kara plucked the spray can from his hand. "This could be dangerous."

Laugh lines appeared around his mouth. "I have some ideas."

The playful side of Ty had always gotten to her.

"I just bet you do."

"Wanna try 'em?" He edged toward her, his words light, his eyes full of hope and longing.

The question hung on the summer night, playful but serious. Kara swallowed a million butterflies. "This is not a good idea."

"Scared?"

"Terrified."

At her admission, Ty drew her into his arms and kissed her. Not a wild and passionate kiss, but tender and earnest. "I'm trying to make a statement here, darlin'. Can't you hear my heart talking?" He took her hand and laid it in the center of his chest. "I'm dying inside because of what your husband did to you. Let me show you how a real man loves."

Love. The word caught her off guard. She tried to think, tried to remember all the reasons she shouldn't be here doing this with Ty Murdock. But nothing came to mind. Somehow, her mind shut down and her heart took over.

Much later, soaking wet from the creek, the taste and scent of Redi-Whip lingering on their lips and bodies, Ty and Kara lay in each other's arms on the quilt. During their lovemaking, Ty had been all the things she remembered. Playful, passionate and incredibly tender. So tender, she'd wept with joy.

Ty stirred and nuzzled her shoulder, his deep drawl lazy and satisfied. "You asleep?"

She stroked his arm, letting her fingers tickle across

the dark skin. "You're the one that always fell asleep."

"Poor man's sedative. Knocks a guy right out." His tongue traced small circles on her neck, sending shock waves clear to her toenails.

"Then why are you awake?"

"Why would I want to be unconscious when I finally have you where I want you?"

"Am I?" A ripple of happiness fluttered through her.

"Where you should have always been. Here, with me, as my woman."

"So you meant it?"

"Meant what?"

"That you never stopped thinking about me."

"Nah, I just said that to get you in bed."

"Ty!" Kara thrust his arm away and sat up. Moonlight gilded her nude body.

Ty pulled her down beside him, expression serious. "I meant every single word. I want us to be a family. Me, you, Lane. A real family." Ty pointed north. "See that star up there?"

"Polaris." He stroked her arm, trailing his fingers up and down over the smooth, damp flesh. She trembled in response.

"Our star, remember?" The words rumbled quietly in Ty's chest.

"We made a million wishes on that star."

Ty shifted position, rolling his head to look at her. "Did you know I named the ranch Star M after those memories?"

Surprised, Kara answered, "I thought…"

Ty hugged her close to his side. "You thought I

was the most conceited rodeo cowboy that ever won a belt buckle.''

"Yeah, I guess I did.''

"You had a right.'' He sighed, a heavy, achingly sad sound so unlike him. "I wish I'd never left you. Or that you'd come with me. All my life I fought against being like my daddy, and then I walked out on you just like he did us.''

"We weren't married. Your father was. That makes a difference.''

He put a hand on either side of her face, pushing back the damp locks that tumbled onto his chest. "If we had been, that psycho wouldn't have hurt you, and Lane would be my son, not Josh Riddley's. If it's any consolation to you, I suffered over that. Knowing you'd had another man's baby tore me up.''

Emotions tumbled like tennis shoes in a clothes dryer, thumping and banging inside her. Had she made the ultimate mistake by not telling Ty about his own son?

Tell him, a voice inside screamed. *Tell him now.* But fear ruled her, and she kept silent. They had just begun to find their way back to each other, and she was so afraid of losing him again. He believed Lane was Josh's son. If he discovered the truth, he'd see her as something much worse than a liar—he'd see her as the woman who'd kept his son away from him. Trust, once broken, was a hard thing to regain. She should know.

"Josh Riddley is out of my life forever. Let's leave it that way.''

"He worries me, Kara. There's this nagging voice in the back of my head that says sooner or later, Riddley will cause trouble." He traced the curve of her cheekbone with one finger.

He couldn't be as worried as she was. "The adoption papers are signed and filed," Kara reminded him, her stomach knotting. "Lane will be your legal son and heir. Josh can't do anything."

"I know how I'd feel if I had a son and his mother tried to keep him away from me."

Pulse pounding, Kara asked, "How? How would you feel?"

"Cheated. Furious. A man has as much right to his own flesh and blood as a woman does."

That was exactly what she'd feared. Even the sweet sedation of their love couldn't block out the truth. Ty would hate her if he ever found out that Lane was his son. She'd kept them apart for five years.

The truth hung in the air with the faint remnants of candle smoke, just waiting to be revealed. The burden of her deceit weighed heavily on Kara. Ty needed to know. He deserved to know. But she was too afraid of losing him to admit the truth.

"He's a great kid." Backlit by the moon and stars, he shifted toward her, stirring the scent of roses and casting the shadow of his body over hers. "I'd like to teach him to rodeo."

She hadn't thought it possible to love Ty Murdock any more than she already did. "If he wants to rodeo, he should learn from the best."

"Thanks for that." She felt his smile as he placed his lips against her cheek. "There's something else I want to ask you."

"About Lane?" Her pulse quickened. Would it always be this way? Would she forever be afraid when they discussed their son?

"No, not about Lane. About the rodeo."

"What about it?"

"I want to ride in the Ft. Worth bull brawl at the end of the month."

Panic rose in Kara like hot lava, all out of proportion to the situation. "No. Absolutely not."

"The prize money's incredible, Kara. Enough to buy that herd bull we need, with some left over."

"But what if something happens?" She sat up and pivoted to look into his eyes. Moonlight reflected on the black orbs, shining with eagerness for his other love. Fear knotted in her throat. "What if you get hurt?"

Ty stroked her jaw, his touch light, loving, reassuring. "Hey, darlin', I'm a better cowboy than that."

"Even great cowboys get hurt. Sometimes they get killed."

"Nothing is going to happen. I promise." He smiled his best cowboy smile and pulled at her. "Now, lie back down here and let's find that can of whipped cream."

Kara slapped his hands away. "You set me up, didn't you? All this—the picnic, the romance—you got what you wanted just like before, and now you're leaving me again."

"No!" He yanked her hard against his chest. "I care about you, Kara. I didn't know you'd be so upset about one little rodeo."

"The last time you drove off to a rodeo, I didn't see you for six years. Can you understand that?"

"Not this go-round. I'm not leaving you behind. You and Lane are going to Ft. Worth with me."

The strong thud of his heart resounded against her body. "I'm afraid, Ty. Maybe it doesn't make sense to you, but I have this feeling that something terrible will happen at that rodeo.''

''And I have the feeling that I'll win, darlin'. I know what I'm doing. I'm good at it, and the prize money is phenomenal. Every bull rider in five states will be there.''

Every bull rider in five states. Rodeo was a very small world, and Josh Riddley was a bull rider. The rope of tension tightened.

Her arms circled his neck, and she clung to him in a way that was so uncharacteristic of the independent woman she'd become. ''I can't lose you again.''

''Darlin', we need this money for *us,* for our future.'' Smoothing her hair back, he lifted her face and kissed her brow. ''Stop worrying. Nothing is gonna happen.''

He was a bull rider, a good one, and if his mind was made up to earn some money this way, she'd have to let him go. But the unreasonable worry wouldn't leave her alone. Something terrible was going to happen at that rodeo, and she was helpless to stop it.

Chapter Eleven

A near capacity crowd milled around the Cowboy Coliseum in Ft. Worth, buying T-shirts emblazoned with pro-rodeo logos and snacking on nachos and giant pretzels. Several cowgirls in incredibly tight red Roper jeans and low-necked blouses hawked programs in the lobby. Kara bought one, the second she'd purchased in the past twenty-four hours. An overexcited Lane had spilled pop on the first one the night before when Ty had ridden his bull in the first go-round.

"Can I have some cotton candy, Mama?" Lane asked from beneath his cowboy hat.

"Then you'll need something to drink." She tucked the program beneath one arm and smiled a knowing, mother's smile at Ty, who ambled along beside them. "And after the pop you'll need to go to the bathroom again."

"Ah, Kara, what's a rodeo without cotton candy and pop." Ty stopped in front of one of the countless vendors, bought the snacks and handed them to a grinning Lane along with a handful of change.

"Thanks, Ty." Lane looked at Kara with dark, solemn eyes. "I promise I won't go to the bathroom during the bull riding. Okay?"

"You two." Shaking her head, Kara lifted her hands in surrender. "I don't stand a chance, do I?"

"Nope." Ty winked at the smiling five-year-old.

"Nope." Lane imitated, and stretched his small legs out as far as he could to keep pace with Ty's much longer ones. He added a cocky swagger, doing his best to perfect his hero's walk. "You gonna ride that ol' bull tonight, Ty?"

"Gonna do my best, partner."

"You're the best bull rider in the whole world, ain't ya?"

"Aren't you," Kara corrected automatically as she listened to the conversation between Ty and their son. He was a wonderful father. He'd taken Lane into his care as though they'd always been together, and there was nothing but love in the way the boy responded. That she'd allowed fear and insecurity to keep them apart so long filled her with guilt.

Dressed in performance gear, Ty Murdock was splendid, and more than one female turned to watch him walk through the lobby on his way to the bucking chutes. Dressed in black and silver, he shone like a star in the night sky. He wore the belt buckle that proclaimed him a champion and a number on his back that marked him as a competitor. But it was the leather chaps, flapping above the shiny, jingling spurs that filled Kara's heart. The Star M logo worked into the fine leather below each knee said he'd had her in his heart every time he'd climbed aboard a bull. She prayed he'd never regret that devotion.

"Intermission's about over." Ty paused at the ramp and nudged his chin upward. "You two better head on back to your seats and get ready."

Ty was as relaxed and confident as she'd ever seen him. He'd laughed and joked all day, reliving the good ride of the night before and promising her a steak dinner with all the trimmings after he won tonight. He didn't seem the least bit afraid of what might happen in the arena.

"How long till you ride, Ty?" Lane wrapped his tongue around the blue cotton candy. A piece stuck to the end of his nose. He peeled it off and folded it into his mouth.

"Won't be long now." Ty scuffed Lane's hat and patted his back. "Cheer for me and wave your hat. I'll be looking right at you after the ride."

A surge of adrenaline hit Kara with the force of a linebacker. She'd fought her nerves all week. Even though the first round had gone off without a hitch, she couldn't shake the foreboding that nagged at her.

"Ty," she started, trying to still the trembling that suddenly overtook her body. Cowboys were a superstitious lot. She didn't want to jinx him by whining and clinging, but he had to know she loved him before he went in that arena. She swallowed hard and forced herself to smile. "Good luck out there." She touched his cheek. "I love you."

He looked stunned. "You do?"

"More than you'll ever know."

Ty swooped her against his chest and kissed her hard. "Then quit your worrying, woman. Everything's going to be just fine.'' He rubbed his nose against hers and laughed. ''Eight seconds to the money.''

Eight seconds. In the movie *Eight Seconds,* the cowboy died.

Kara buried her face against his neck, inhaled the warm scent that was his and his alone, and shut out the unsettling voice. A bull rider's wife had to put on a brave act.

''Ride 'im, cowboy,'' she whispered, fear choking her. She waited for him to amble behind the chutes before taking Lane by the hand and heading into the arena.

If Kara hadn't been so nervous about this whole thing, Ty would have whistled. She loved him! Surprised jubilation swelled in his chest. Everyone would soon realize he was man enough to settle down. He and Kara were actually going to make this marriage work. He felt it in his bones, just the way he felt about his chances for a clean ride tonight. It had always been this way for him. If his gut said he was in the money, then he was. Kara was a rodeo performer. She knew how it worked. He was still mystified that she had reacted so negatively about the whole thing. Must just be bad memories from when he'd been gone and she'd gotten involved with Riddley. Last night in the hotel she'd tossed and turned half the night. He shook his head. There was no reason for her to be scared. No reason at all.

Strutting confidently to the back of the chutes, the memory of her declaration buoying him, Ty's boot made contact with something. He looked down. A paper cup sailed across the concrete and slammed into a wall. Some of his jauntiness fled. A paper cup. Why did he have to kick a paper cup? Not that he was superstitious, but to a cowboy, kicking a paper cup before a ride was worse than having a black cat cross your path. It was a very bad omen.

He had the sudden urge to rush back to Kara for one last good luck kiss. A quick glance toward the chutes told him there was plenty of time. He stared another second at the empty beer cup, then headed up the ramp to find his wife and let her know he would be fine. Just fine.

As they made their way down the concourse toward their seats near the arena floor, Kara smiled at Lane clomping happily along in his boots. His constant chatter helped divert her thoughts from Ty's upcoming ride.

"Mama, I need to go to the bathroom."

"Lane!" she cried in exasperation. "You promised to wait until after the bull riding."

He jigged up and down, sloshing the ice in his empty cup. "I can't help it. I gotta."

With a sigh of surrender, Kara took the cup, tossed it into the trash and led Lane to the nearest restroom. She was waiting just outside, holding the soggy blue cotton candy in one hand and the program in the other when a man came out of the restroom.

Her worst nightmare had come to life. Josh Riddley spotted her immediately and moved in her direction.

"Well, lookie here what I found." The slur told her he'd been drinking. If Lane hadn't been in the rest-room she'd have run like a cutting horse. Instead, she gritted her teeth and faced her ex-husband.

"Leave me alone, Josh."

"Told you I'd catch-up with you sooner or later."

He slung a limber arm across her shoulders and hugged her against him. "Why don't you come on out to the camper with me?" The smell of beer and smoke hung over him like smog over L.A. Kara shuddered and yanked away, frantically wishing Lane would hurry.

"Don't get snotty with me, woman." Josh backed her against the water fountain and thrust his lower body into hers.

She shoved at his chest. "Get away from me before I start screaming and bring every cowboy in this place down on your head."

"Always was a little too feisty, weren't you? But I know how to take you down a notch or two." Josh slammed his lips over hers. The slimy taste and rancid smell nearly gagged her. Revulsion shuddered through her body as she squirmed and fought against his much superior bulk. She couldn't bear for Lane to see this. It would frighten him to pieces. Just when she was certain she'd vomit, Josh was yanked around and slammed full force into the wall.

"What the hell are you doing to my wife?"

When he'd rounded the corner and seen Kara struggling against some groping cowboy, Ty had lost the cool he worked so hard to keep. A vein throbbed in his temple with such intensity he thought it might be an aneurysm. He grabbed the stranger by the collar with one hand while the other fisted near his nose.

"Your wife?" The drunk's eyes went wide and disbelieving. Then he laughed, an ugly sound, and slumped against the block wall in the exaggerated posture of the moderately drunk. "Well, hell, buddy. Ain't that a coincidence? She's my wife, too."

Ty glanced at Kara. Lane's cotton candy lay smashed at her feet. She was shaking from head to toe, and her bottom lip was puffy. This low-life had to be her ex-husband.

"So you're Riddley," Ty said in disgust, taking the other man's measure and finding him sorely lacking. What had Kara ever seen in this drunken bully?

"Thass right. Whatsit to you?"

Ty tightened his grip on Riddley's shirt collar, perversely pleased when the other man's face mottled a deep red. "You like to get rough with women. Let's see how tough you are with a man."

Kara sprang into action beside him. "Ty, no. He's not worth it. Come on, please." She tugged at his arm. "Go in the rest room and check on Lane. He's been in there too long."

Ty shot her a look, but never moved. Her trembling voice was enough to make him want to hurt this guy real bad. "He owes you an apology, and unless you get it, I'm going to knock his teeth loose."

"She's the one who does the owing." Riddley pushed at Ty's hand, momentarily loosening his stranglehold. "Not many men would take in somebody else's kid like I did."

Ty froze; his heart stopped beating. "What are you talking about?"

"Her kid. Lane. She didn't want no one to know she'd had the little bastard, so I took him in. Let everyone think he was mine."

Inside the arena the crowd roared, but a louder roaring filled Ty's ears. "He's not your son?"

"Is that what she told you?" Riddley laughed, the ugly, snide laugh of someone who enjoys the pain of others. "Well, here's news for you, big shot. I don't know who knocked her up, but it wasn't me."

Ever so slowly Ty's hands fell to his sides, the shock of Riddley's words too great to take in. What was he saying? That Lane belonged to some other man? But who? There hadn't been that much time between his own leaving and Kara's marriage to Riddley.

A cold fear prickled over his skin, lifting the hairs on the back of his neck. He had a vision of Lane, eyes sparkling like black diamonds, his mouth turned up in an ornery grin. Black eyes. Eyes like his own.

"Oh, my God. Oh, my God." Realization struck him like a fist. Why hadn't he seen it before? The eyes, the walk, the tilt of the head. He'd seen them all in his own mirror. Lane was his son, not Riddley's. Lane was his own flesh and blood, and Kara had kept them apart.

Ty battled for control, but the hurt and fury inside him was fast taking over. His hands shook with the need for release. He wanted to hurt somebody—and Riddley was handy. He'd called Lane a bastard. That was enough to kill him for. His anger mounted to the boiling point. If he didn't turn around and walk away now, he'd do something stupid. He waited two beats, narrowed his eyes…and did something stupid. Riddley went down like an imploded building.

Lane chose that moment to emerge from the rest room.

"Mama, I dropped my quarter in the potty."

Quickly, Kara pulled the child against her stomach, shielding him from the ugly scene. All around them people gathered in a semicircle to stare. Murmurs of shock reverberated through the crowd.

A lanky cowboy broke through and grabbed Ty from behind.

"Hey, Murdock, you're up next." He gazed from Ty to the man on the ground. "What's going on down here?"

Ty shook him off. "I'll be there in a minute, Jeb."

"That maniac nearly broke my jaw," Riddley complained, rubbing at the blood trickling from his lip.

"I've known this boy for a long time, mister, and I ain't never seen him mad," Jeb said, his own fists doubling. "If you done riled him up, you better get your tail on out of here before the rest of us jump on you."

Riddley scrambled to his feet and lurched toward the exit, but Ty paid him no mind. His gaze was riveted on Kara. Her face was the color of paste. He held her eyes with his, trying to understand, trying to see things from her perspective. In the end he failed.

"Later," he said, jabbing a finger at her. "You've got a lot of explaining to do."

Turning on his heel, Ty stalked toward the bucking chute, so full of hurt and fury, he wanted to strangle someone. Hitting Riddley hadn't been anywhere near enough.

Lane was his son, and because of Kara's deceit, he'd missed five years of the boy's life. Five years! She'd forced him to do the one thing he'd vowed never to do—abandon his own child the way his father had abandoned him. How could she have done that to him? Had it been her way of punishing him? And why hadn't she told him the truth after they married? She knew he was crazy about Lane. Jiminy, he'd given her plenty of chances to tell him. He'd even admitted how much he wished the boy was his own. Still she'd cruelly kept his own child a secret from him.

A red snorting Brahma with eighteen-inch hooking horns thrashed in the chute. Two cowboys, riding the edge of the pen, struggled to control him. Though Ty was almost numb with shock and pain, he had a bull to ride. He waited until the creature calmed the slightest bit, then he eased himself onto the massive back and started his wrap. Normally, he settled for a simple wrap. Tonight he didn't care. He was going to ride this bull if it killed him. Kara hadn't wanted him to, and by all that was holy, he'd ride it just to show her. Grabbing the rope, he began the suicide wrap. Palm up, he yanked the rope tighter and tighter over his leather gloved hand.

He hardly felt the tense two thousand pounds of mad muscle between his legs. His mind pounded with the bitter truth. Kara had deceived him in the worst way possible. She'd stolen five years of time with his son.

From the public address system, he heard his name announced. "Out of chute number seven, a mighty fine Texas cowboy we haven't seen for a while, Ty Murdock. He made a good showing last night, scoring an eighty-two. Tonight he's drawn Rowdy, a rank bull that's only been ridden once this year."

The voice droned on, but Ty shut it out and tried to concentrate. Anything but total focus on the bull could get a man killed real quick. But once again, the churning inside pushed to the front. She'd deceived him. Lied to him. And all he'd done was love her. The truth hurt so much, he thought his chest would explode.

"Whenever you're ready, cowboy," a quiet voice beside him said.

Vision blurred, heart pounding for all the wrong reasons, Ty locked his thighs around the bull's wide body, nodded his head, and the gate clattered open.

Kara clenched the arms of her arena seat and prayed like she'd never prayed before. A mountain of furious bull shot from gate seven, twisting and twirling in a terrifying ballet.

Kara's pulse leaped into action, pounding the guilt and fear deeper and deeper into her consciousness. If anything happened to Ty during his ride, she would be responsible.

The crowd around her faded. She was aware of the screaming, the fans on their feet, but everything within her was focused on the wildly thrashing bull and the man on his back. Rowdy was a fearsome opponent, his powerful back end whipping from side to side while his hind legs kicked skyward. Ty remained positioned over his hand, strong thighs gripping the animal's side. The Star M logo flapped madly against Rowdy's red hide.

Few cowboys could stay aboard when an animal changed directions. As Rowdy tossed his massive horns back to the right, Ty's body slipped sideways. Kara sucked in a frightened breath, aware that she was now on her feet. If Ty lost control now, he'd fall helplessly beneath the rampaging animal.

Using his free hand, Ty pumped the air, working his way back to the middle. Like a man with no caution, he raked his spurs along Rowdy's sides. The bull responded with another wild turn. This time Ty maintained his balance, his body swinging with the rhythm of his opponent.

When the buzzer sounded, the crowd erupted in a roar of approval.

"A phenomenal ride from Ty Murdock," the announcer boomed. Kara closed her eyes and wilted into her seat, shaking violently from the adrenaline rush. He was safe. Thank God. Thank God.

"Mama, Ty can't get off."

Her son's words were like a gunshot. She bolted up from the chair, grappling to hold on to her sanity. Ty was hung up, the worst possible scenario for a bull-rider. Normally when a cowboy dismounts, the rope binding him to the bull's back flies free. This time the rope tangled, ensnaring Ty's hand while the rest of his body hung helplessly over the animal's side.

Out on the dirt floor of the arena, the wild bull thrashed and bucked, tossing his massive horns at the dangling rider. One well-place swipe could fracture Ty's skull or puncture a lung. Hanging by one arm, Ty flopped like a rag doll, at the mercy of the bull and the bullfighting clowns who had leaped into action. Even if they managed to free him, he could fall help-lessly beneath the hooves of 2,000 pounds of stomp-ing, hooking fury.

Kara's first impulse was to rush onto the floor and fight the raging animal with her bare hands. She moved toward the aisle but stopped when Lane's ter-rified voice called to her.

"Mama, Ty's getting hurt. Ty's getting hurt."

She couldn't lose it in front of Lane. No matter what happened she must be strong for him. Hands trem-bling, mouth so dry her throat ached, Kara pulled her son onto her lap and watched the horrible drama play out.

One clown distracted the bull by bravely grabbing

the fearsome horns. Another jumped onto the animal, yanking frantically at the bullrope holding Ty prisoner. When the rope gave, Ty tumbled to the ground...and lay still. Two cowboys rushed to his aid while the bullfighters urged the kicking bull out the gate.

"Why don't he get up, Mama?" Lane sounded as small and frightened as Kara felt.

"He will. He will." *Please God, let him get up. I've hurt him so much. Please give me another chance to do things right.*

Dust still swirling around them, the assisting cowboys knelt at each side of Ty. Others had started into the arena. Before they could reach the fallen rider, he stirred, struggling upward. The two cowboys gripped his arms and brought him to his feet. He looked dazed and wobbly, and blood ran from his lip and nose. Someone handed him his black Stetson just as the PA system blared his score.

"There's your winner, ladies and gentlemen. Eighty-eight points for a mighty fine ride from one tough cowboy, Ty Murdock."

Ty shook himself free of his helpers. With his right shoulder oddly lower than the other, he lifted his hat in his left hand and waved it toward the erupting crowd. Very slowly he turned until he faced the section where Lane and Kara were waiting. His searching gaze locked onto Kara's for one eternal moment before dropping to Lane. Then he replaced his hat and strode out of the arena.

Chapter Twelve

Ty knew the trip home would be miserable for more than one reason. His shoulder ached like a son-of-gun and his heart ached worse than that. Kara sat on the passenger side of the truck looking like a horse had kicked her in the gut while his son sat between them. His son. The very thought of Lane being his own flesh-and-blood child set a hundred different emotions shooting off inside him like fireworks on the Fourth of July. He couldn't get over it. Lane was his baby boy. If he hadn't been so stunned and hurt over Kara's lies, he'd have whooped for joy.

"Shouldn't we go by the hospital and have that shoulder looked at?" Kara asked, her voice tentative.

Even in the shadowy glow of the streetlights, he could see how pale her face was. He didn't want to feel bad for her. He didn't even want to talk to her. Couldn't talk to her just yet. Not in front of his son, anyway. The ache rising up in his chest was too powerful and the anger rising with it just might make him say something he'd regret forever.

Using his left hand, he eased the shifter down and pulled slowly out of the parking lot. Kara heaved a heavy sigh and stared out over the dashboard at the line of cars exiting the coliseum, their headlights peering into the darkness.

Ever so gently Lane placed one small hand on Ty's arm. "Want me to rub it for you?" he offered, dark eyes filled with compassion.

Everything inside Ty seized upward as he looked down at the small hand. How many times had he missed out on that kind of sweetness all because Kara had chosen to keep this boy a secret from his own father?

"It's okay, partner," he said, reassuringly. "The doc fixed me up behind the chutes." He gave what he hoped was a convincing wink. No sense in the little guy worrying about him. "Popped that sucker right back in place. It'll be sore, that's all."

Just the same, Lane's small fingers kneaded Ty's much larger biceps. Ty ached from the tenderness of it—the son comforting the father. How many times had Lane needed his comfort when he hadn't been there to give it? Regret pulsed through him in waves strong enough to drown in.

"Did you win?"

Ty gave a short laugh. Somehow the win didn't seem nearly as important now as it had a few hours ago. "First in the go-round, second in the average."

Lane squirmed against his seat belt, angling his body toward Ty so that he could slide both hands up and down the injured shoulder. "Is that good?"

"Not a bad payday." Enough to do the things he

and Kara had discussed, though now his heart wasn't in buying bulls and building stock pens. Right then he didn't know where his heart was, but it wasn't on the ranch he'd planned to share with Kara.

"Enough money to buy me a new saddle?"

"Lane!" Kara admonished from her hiding spot in the dark corner of the truck. "Don't ask people to buy you things."

Ty stiffened, the pain inside him turning to anger. He wasn't other people. He was the boy's father. Even now, when he knew the truth, she shut him out.

"You can ask me for anything, little partner," he muttered through clenched teeth. "Anything, anytime."

From the corner of his eye, he saw Kara cross her arms and sink back into the corner. Let her fret. She'd done this. She was going to have to live with it.

Lane shot a quick look at his mother. When she didn't protest further, he said, "A saddle with a Star M on it would look mighty fine on my panimillo."

Ty smiled sadly. Lane was doing his best to talk like a cowboy. He wouldn't have to be an imitation if he'd always been where he belonged. "I'll think on it, Lane."

The child sighed, seemingly satisfied with that answer. With his legs too short to touch the floor, his boots stuck straight out from the seat. He studied the tapping toes of his black boots and admitted, "I was scared when you was flopping. I didn't care if you won or not, just so's you didn't get killed."

He wished the boy hadn't seen that. Scary sight to a five-year-old. Gingerly, he draped the sore arm around Lane's shoulders. "I was scared, too," he admitted. If nothing else, he could give Lane his honesty. It was more than Kara had done.

"You was?"

"A bull's a dangerous animal. Any man who says he's not scared is lying."

"It scared Mama, too. She started crying."

Ty took his attention from the road long enough to steal a glance at Kara. She kept her gaze riveted out the side window as though the cars and trucks passing at killer speed on the dark four-lane highway held the answer to life's mysteries. She looked as forlorn as a motherless calf. He fought the awful urge to tell her it was all right, that he understood. But, he didn't understand. She'd intentionally kept him away from his son and spun a web of lies to keep them apart.

"Did *you* cry?" Ty asked the earnest upturned face.

"Granddad said big boys don't cry."

"Your granddaddy's smart about lots of things." His mind more on the child than driving, Ty automatically decelerated as the four lane narrowed to two. "But he's wrong about that."

"You won't think I'm a sissy if I cry sometimes when I get hurt or something?"

"Crying won't make you a sissy, son." The word of kinship slipped out of his mouth as easy and naturally as if he'd always used it. "Sometimes boys need to cry real bad. Maybe they don't do it where anyone else can see 'em, but if they're smart, they'll go on ahead and let it out."

"Did you cry when the bull flopped you around?"

"No. Not then. I was way too busy trying to get loose."

"But it hurt, didn't it?"

"Yeah." He glanced over at Kara. "It hurt a lot."

He couldn't tell a child that lots of things in life hurt worse than getting hung-up on a bull.

"Do you ever cry?"

"Sometimes." He sure felt like crying now, and if he didn't find a way to shift this conversation, he just might do it. Easing the sore arm to the radio, he caught the strains of a country station, turned it low and let the sad tunes stoke the pain throbbing inside him.

Kara stood in the doorway of the bedroom, the knot in her stomach tight and hot. Since the moment Ty had come out of the rodeo arena, she'd felt his hurt, his confusion. All the way from Ft. Worth, he'd carefully avoided any conversation with her. Gone was the jaunty grin, the teasing eyes, the tender hands. The husband who'd wooed and adored her looked liked a Texas thunderhead about to erupt. Worse than that. He looked like someone had murdered his best friend. His eyes were so black the pupils disappeared, and his mouth was a grim line. The slow, controlled way he removed his boots and placed his hat on the bed said it all. He was devastated…and furious.

He emptied the change from his pocket and tossed the envelope with his winnings on the dresser. Kara thought her heart might burst when he removed a blue feather from one pocket, stroked it between thumb and finger, then placed it next to the envelope with his winnings. Lane had given him the prized blue feather as a good-luck charm.

Finally he heaved a shuddering sigh, rotated his bad shoulder and turned to look at her with eyes the color of black ice. With a tilt of his head, he motioned her into the room and closed the door behind them. With

Lane safely tucked into bed, the moment of truth had arrived.

"When were you going to tell me?" Barely concealed anger teetered around the edges of his voice.

What could she say—what could anyone say—that would make him understand? He was hurt, angry, and he had every right to be.

She gulped back the rising fear.

"I wanted to tell you." Tentatively she reached out, laying a conciliatory hand on his chest, making a connection between her heart and his, hoping against all hope that he'd feel her regret. Beneath her palm, his chest rose and fell in agitation. He stared down at her for one heartbeat, then backed away and let her hand slide into nothingness. Some of Kara's hope fell with it.

"If you wanted to tell me so badly, why didn't you? Why the charade?" He gave a short, mirthless laugh. "I even told you how much I wished Lane was my child, and still you lied."

"I never lied." She crossed her arms, rubbing at the sudden chill creeping over her flesh.

"Five years, Kara." He jabbed a finger at her. "Five years I've been a father, and you didn't bother to tell me."

Her legs began to tremble. She eased down on the bed, gripping the familiar blue comforter. Tears clogged her throat. "I was too afraid."

"Of what?" Both his arms flew out, palms up, in disbelief. He tipped his fingers backward, pointing at himself. "Of me?"

"No. Yes." She'd never feared him physically. Not Ty. Such violence wasn't in him. But she had been afraid for what he could do—and had done—to her heart. "You have to realize something, Ty. You had left me. Everyone said you'd taken up with Shannon Sullivan."

"And you believed them. You thought I was a chip off the old block, a carbon copy of my old man." Ty shook his head, his voice bitter.

"You had left me," she cried, desperate to get through to him. "I thought you didn't want me anymore."

Walking to the window, Ty stared out, his back to Kara. He gripped the window frame on each side. "I called. Why didn't you tell me then?"

"Because I thought they were guilt calls. Calls to reassure yourself that I was fine, so you didn't have to feel responsible for breaking my heart."

He spun around, jaw tight. "That's bull, and you know it."

"I didn't know it then. All I knew was that you were gone. My mama was only six months in the grave. I was pregnant and confused and terrified." She rose from the bed and started toward him. "For my daddy to know that I'd failed him so miserably would have put him in the ground with Mama."

"You never did give your dad enough credit," he spat. "What did you think he would do? Disown you?"

"You know my daddy's pride. He wouldn't have been able to hold his head up in this county with people gossiping about his daughter. He thought I hung the moon, and wanted everyone else to believe it, too. I couldn't hurt him that way."

"Girls have babies without husbands all the time."

"Not Taylors."

Tilting his head back, he let out an exasperated sigh.

"You and that insufferable Taylor pride. You weren't worried about letting your daddy down. You were worried about yourself, about keeping that image of perfection Pete had of you. The rodeo queen, the honor student, the girl who never caused her parents one bit of grief." With one hand kneading his shoulder, he shook his head. "I've got news for you, Kara. That pride has cost you a lot more than it's ever given in return."

A dull ache had started in Kara's temples. Could Ty be right? Had she misjudged her father and now mortally wounded her marriage to perpetuate some misguided myth about herself? Was she that shallow? That cruel? The dull ache spread behind her eyes. Squeezing them closed, she pressed both thumbs into the sockets.

"Think about it, Kara. If you'd told me the truth from the start, I would have come running home as fast as a lost dog. You and my son," his stare accused her, "would never have been abused by Josh Riddley. This ranch would never have fallen into such disrepair because Pete was too brokenhearted to care about it anymore. And—" he paused long enough for her to look up "—you wouldn't be losing your second husband."

The world tilted. The headache became a throbbing drumbeat. She moved toward him.

"Ty, please." If she had to beg, she would. She reached for him. He backed away, but she kept her hand out, beseeching.

A vein pulsed over Ty's left eye. He shook his head, the expression on his face one of such agony it pierced Kara's conscience. She'd done this to him. To them.

"Trust is everything, Kara. Without it, a marriage

is an empty shell. Everything we have is built on lies. I don't want that. I can't live that way.''

"Lane is the only thing I ever kept from you, Ty. Everything else is true and real.''

"How can I ever know what's true and what isn't?''

"I love you. Surely you believe that.''

"Love? You loved me so much you put me through the process of adopting my own son?'' He shook his head sadly. Despair hung on him like an oversize shirt. "That's not my idea of love.''

"We can get through this. Please, Ty, I never wanted this to happen.''

"Neither did I, but you made the decision without me.'' He took his hat from the foot of the bed and studied the curving brim, his handsome face sick with sorrow. "Which do you want? The ranch? Or Lane?''

Kara rocked back, stunned that he would even ask. He wanted her gone, no matter what the price. He hated her, just as she'd feared he would. Her fairy-tale marriage was over, her dreams shattered, all because she hadn't had the courage to tell him the truth. The knowledge blew through her like a sharp wind on a very cold day. She'd had it all and thrown it away.

"You know the answer to that. Lane and I will leave in the morning,'' she offered quietly.

A huge, shuddering sigh issued from Ty's chest. "God, this hurts. I love him. I need to be his father. And he needs me.''

Hope flared in Kara's heart. "I'll never keep anything from you again, I promise.''

"I wish I could believe that.'' Holding her gaze with an intense black stare, he shook his head slowly. "I wish I could. But I can't.''

It was over. Really over. She'd killed any hope of

love between them. Kara swallowed the hysteria that
wanted to erupt. If she let go of it now, she'd lose her
mind. If nothing else, she'd leave with her pride intact.
Swiping at her sodden face, she gulped back the fresh
threat of bitter tears and wrapped her pride around her
like a protective cloak. With all the strength she could
muster, she offered an olive branch.

"You and Lane deserve to know each other. I'll
bring him to visit as often as I can."

"Yeah. Right."

With a bitter smile he twisted the doorknob and
walked out of Kara's life for the second time. This
time forever.

Chapter Thirteen

Ty sat on the back porch, looking up at the dark sky, more lonely than he'd ever been in his life. Everything around him served as a reminder of all he'd had and all he'd lost. Kara was gone. His boy was gone. The four days seemed like an eternity. The freshly painted red barn, the little purple flowers she'd planted all around the back porch—shoot, even the apple scent in the bathroom screamed Kara's name. With a heavy sigh he stuck his head in his hands and wondered how his life had gone to hell in a handbasket.

"Lies," he muttered to the wooden porch step between his knees. "Nothing but lies."

Kara had lied to him about the most fundamentally important thing in a man's life.

At the soft swish of feet on grass, he looked up and saw Pete coming at him across the yard.

"Figured you'd be sitting out here."

"House is pretty empty."

"Yep. Big ol' place like this is meant for family."

Shifting his weight to his good leg, Pete gripped the porch post and leaned against it.

"Kara ruined that." Funny how he could tell Pete such a thing about his own daughter, but that was the way things had always been between them. He talked. Pete listened.

"You found out about the young'un, I guess."

Surprised, Ty looked at Pete's weathered face, bathed a hazy yellow from the kitchen light shining through the window. Kara had worked so hard to spare Pete's feelings.

"How long have you known?"

"Didn't really. Just guessed. I know my Kara Dean. She wouldn't go off and have another man's baby the way she felt about you. After a while it all added up. Then when I seen you and the boy together..." He patted at his shirt pocket for the familiar can of tobacco. "Hell, anybody with eyes could see Lane belonged to you."

The irony wasn't lost on Ty. Pete had seen it. Why hadn't he? "Why didn't you say something?"

Pete studied the round can as he tapped it against his palm. "Figured she had her reasons for keeping it to herself, and I knowed you'd pitch a fit when you found out. Can't say as I blame you, but I was hoping the two of you could see your way to make things right again."

Suddenly a lot of things started to make sense. The ranch was falling apart and needed Ty's skills. Pete wanted Kara to move home, but was too proud to ask. He knew the history between Ty and Kara, and suspecting the truth about Lane and thought they should make things right. "You knew very well Kara wouldn't stand by and watch me take over this ranch without a fight. You set this whole thing up, didn't you?''

A slight smile tipped Pete's lips as he opened the snuff can and released the aroma of wintergreen. ''Things did seem to fall together, didn't they?''

''And now they've fallen apart.'' Ty pulled a handful of weeds from around the step and sifted them one by one through his fingers.

''Nothing that can't be remedied.''

''She lied to me, Pete,'' Ty said bitterly. Tossing the grass to one side, he swiped a hand down the leg of his jeans. ''She kept my own son away from me.''

Considering, Pete stuffed a pinch of tobacco behind his bottom lip, recapped the can and put it in his shirt pocket. ''I ain't condoning what she did, but there's always two sides to look at. After you took off, don't you reckon she was scared?''

''I would have come back for her. Didn't she know that?''

''Maybe she would have if half the town hadn't told her you was just like your daddy and she'd never see you again.''

The old bitterness rose in Ty's chest. ''I'm not my old man.''

''I knowed that. But when that Sullivan gal came into town swishing her tail and blabbering on about the two of you, telling things no decent woman would tell, you was fodder for every old gossip around.''

''I never did a thing with Shannon. I swear it.''

''Heck, boy, I knowed that, too. Think I'd want you as a son-in-law if I believed any of that business? The trouble was, Kara Dean believed it. There she was having your baby, and you was gone. Her mama was gone. And she was scared to death of disappointing me. I guess she was just plain scared.''

Ty had a sudden flash of the day he'd left. Kara was crying, and he'd driven away and left her in his dust. Though he'd loved her, he'd been young and selfish, thinking the world—and the woman—would stop and wait for him. But some things couldn't wait.

''I want to tell you something, boy.'' Pete went on talking to the darkness, his face lifted toward the heavens. ''Life is short, a vapor, the Good Book says. Every minute you spend fussing with the people you love is a minute you'll regret when they're gone.''

The power of the old man's words crashed down on Ty like a bad bull ride. For six years Kara had had no reason at all to believe he loved her enough to take care of their baby. Six long, wasted years, that were as much his fault as hers. Even after coming back to the Tilted T, he'd given her nothing but a marriage of convenience, holding back that little part of him that might want to leave.

Now, with all that was within him, he wanted to stay, but only if Kara was by his side. All his adult life he'd tried hard not to be like his father. He wanted to be there for his kids, to give them the love and stability that had been missing in his own life. But tonight his son—and the woman he loved—was in Oklahoma. He sat here brooding in Texas while life ticked away. And this time, the separation was his own doing.

Praying he hadn't thrown away their last chance at happiness, he rose and gripped Pete's shoulder, a new determination taking hold. ''Think she'll have me back?''

''A smart man would be finding out.''

After the cruel things he'd said, Kara might not even talk to him, but if there was one chance in a million that she'd try again, he had to take it. He didn't care how far he had to go or what he had to do. As Pete said, they'd already wasted too much of life's precious time. Heart hammering, he bade Pete goodbye and headed to his truck, aiming it toward the North Star...and everything that mattered in his life.

Kara couldn't sleep. Every time she closed her eyes, Ty's face, filled with hurt and disbelief, rose up to haunt her. Pride was cold comfort when her heart and body cried out for the love of her life.

Weary of a jumbled mind that wouldn't shut down no matter how tired she was, Kara threw back the sheet. Taking care not to awaken Marietta or Lane, she carried a Dr. Pepper and a box of Cheez-Its out onto the sidewalk in front of the apartment. The concrete was hot beneath her bare feet. Security lights chased the darkness into the parking area. It was late, but even in this residential section of the city, there was no peace and quiet. Cars roared by, loud music bumping, laughter rippling on the hot, stale air. Sirens wailed in the distance. Eighteen wheelers shifted down, unwinding on the nearby interstate.

She sighed and took a sip of the strong soda, missing the ranch and her loved ones now more than ever. She longed for them with such intensity, she ached. She'd left her heart there, and living with this big, gaping hole in her chest was mighty hard.

"I'm sorry, Murdock," she whispered to the night. "I wish I had been honest from the start. I wish..."

Wishes. For a little while she'd believed in their magic.

Hugging her knees to her chest, she gazed upward, some deep part of her wanting to try just one more time to wring some magic from the stars. To her disappointment, city lights obscured the heavens. The sweeping beacons of searchlights and the red dots of passing planes replaced the constellations.

Even the stars had abandoned her.

A car turned into the parking lot, headlights sweeping across the front of the apartment complex. Kara shrank back, waiting for the high beams to shut off. They didn't.

"Doesn't the idiot know people are trying to sleep?" She rose and gathered her snacks to return inside. Still the high beams glared directly at her. Feeling vulnerable outside all alone, she started in. As her hand touched the doorknob the car lights went out and a door slammed. Jittery, she turned to look. Adrenaline as hot as electricity shot up her spine. A cowboy with a very familiar walk strode across the pavement.

"Kara." He spoke quietly, but the beloved baritone carried on the heat waves.

Ty. Mesmerized, Kara could only stare. What was he doing here? A spark of hope flamed upward but quickly died, replaced by fear and dread. Divorce papers? Or worse, a bid for custody of their son? A trembling started deep inside as she lowered the pop and crackers to the sidewalk.

"You're up late," he said when he'd reached her side, bringing with him the cold from his air conditioner and his own wonderful brand of manly scent. "Everyone okay?"

"Fine." She gripped the iron railing that separated her apartment from the parking lot. *Fine,* she'd said. How stupid to say "fine" when she was dying.

"Can we talk?" He touched her arm, and the old familiar ache that only he could cause welled up in her. Would she ever stop wanting him...needing him...loving him?

Throat thick and dry, she edged away, fearing she'd fall at his feet and beg forgiveness. She'd do it if it would make a difference, but Ty had been very clear, he couldn't forgive. "You drove all this way in the middle of the night to talk?"

"It's important."

"Okay," she motioned to the concrete. "Have a seat."

Ignoring the request, he drew a paper from his pocket and handed it to her. "I brought you something."

"What's this?" She lifted the tri-folded document to the light, but the shadows obscured the words.

"The deed to the Star M."

"The deed?" The words jump-started her pulse. "Why would you do such a thing?" A terrifying thought leaped into her mind as she recalled his parting words: *the ranch or Lane.* Kara spun toward him like a tigress. "You can't have Lane."

"No." Irritated, he waved away the notion. "The deed is signed and notarized. All you have to do is file it at the courthouse in Bootlick, and you and Lane own the Tilted T."

"What happened to the Star M?"

"It's yours. Call it what you like." Removing his Stetson, he stared at it and sighed heavily. "That ranch means nothing to me."

"Nothing?" Kara's heart fell to the hot concrete and shattered into a thousand pieces. The ranch meant nothing...and neither did she. "I see."

"I don't think you do." He reached over and touched her chin, lifting her gaze to his. Onyx eyes pierced her soul. "Do you know how scared I've been of turning out like my dad, scared of not being man enough to stay in one place, scared I'd never have a home and family? Then you and our son made me believe I could take a floundering ranch and make it successful, made me *want* to."

Puzzled, she frowned up at his solemn face. "I don't understand. You just said the ranch meant nothing to you."

"It doesn't. Not this way. Not now." Kara felt the deep tremble in his touch. "Hearing the truth about Lane nearly killed me. All I could think of was how many years I'd missed out on that little boy's sweet love. I felt cheated. But once the anger passed, I had to face the fact that I'm more like my daddy than I wanted to be. I should have listened when you tried to explain why you kept him a secret. I should have understood how scared and hurt you must have been. But I failed you, not once, but twice. That's why the ranch means nothing—because you and Lane aren't there."

The throb of grief in his voice tore her apart. Hope flared like a match in the darkness. "No, Ty. I'm the one who failed by believing you took after your daddy. You may share his blood, but you're nothing like him. Look at the way you took over the ranch to help my dad. And the way you loved and cared for Lane even before you knew he was your son. Sam Murdock would never have done those things. If I hadn't been so self-centered, I'd have seen it all along. You're a good man and a wonderful daddy. Lane misses you terribly."

He took a step closer, black eyes burning intensely. "What about his mama?"

Tossing all her false pride over the railing, Kara admitted, "I was wrong to let fear and pride keep the two of you apart. I've made a lot of mistakes, Ty, but loving you and being loved by you was never one of them. If given the chance I'd do it all over again, only this time I'd be woman enough not to let anything separate us."

Ty closed the distance between them in less time than it took his Stetson to reach the ground. Fiercely he gripped her shoulders and pulled her against him. "Do you mean that? You'd try again? You'd give us another chance to be a family?"

"Yes. Oh, yes." Tears of happiness welled in her eyes. "If you'll forgive me. I never meant to hurt you. I'll never keep anything from you again. I'm so sorry...."

Ty's lips took the apology and turned it to a sigh of pleasure. The touch of his hands stroking her back, her arms, her face, was unbearably tender.

"I love you, darlin'," he whispered against her hair. "Always have. Always will."

"I love you, too." She wound her arms around his trim, hard waist and pressed against him, the rush of euphoria making her light-headed. "Oh, how I wished for this, Ty. With all my heart I wished for one more opportunity to make up for all the hurt I caused you. But tonight, when I searched for our star, it was gone. And I was sure our love had gone with it."

"No, darlin'," Ty's smile was so sweet, Kara's heart skipped a beat. "Our star, like our love, is right where it's always been. We just let the clouds hide it for a while." Drawing her closer, he kissed her with throbbing tenderness. "Let's go wake our boy, Mrs. Murdock, and take him home where he belongs."

"Yes," she replied, tears of joy blurring her vision. "Where we all belong."

Epilogue

Ty reined in the big bay stallion and slid from the saddle just as he spotted her. Blond ponytail bobbing to beat Dixie, Kara stormed across the barnyard with enough energy to power a small country. At the sight Ty's body went on red alert, the surge of desire as fresh as the day a year ago when they'd come home to the Star M for good. With a delighted groan, he quickly unsaddled the stallion, and with a slap on the rump turned him into the lot. Life with Kara was more exhilarating than any bull ride.

"Murdock!"

He grinned to himself, eager to see what she was all stirred up about now. Leaning one elbow on the fence rail, he watched her coming, enjoying every step she took. Even with dusk wrapped around her like a gray cloak, he could see and feel the sparks flying from her vibrant personality.

"Murdock, you've done it again." She stopped six inches away and poked a finger into his chest.

He grabbed the finger, raised it to his lips and kissed it. "What have I done this time?"

"Don't play coy with me, Bubba. You know what you did." Something in her dancing green gaze told him she was more excited than angry. He drew her closer until their bodies touched and her sweet spring scent swirled through his head.

"Okay. I confess. I did it. Now kiss me."

To his delight, she raised on tiptoes, pressed her lips to his and took his breath away.

"Whoa, darlin', whatever I did, tell me so I can be sure to do it again."

"You can't do it again. Not for at least nine months."

Ty's heart forgot to beat. He forgot to breathe. Jiminy Christmas, he forgot who he was. "Are you saying what I think you're saying?"

Impishly she grinned up at him. "Yep, rodeo man, we're going to have another baby."

Ty thought surely he'd die of happiness right on the spot. "And you're blaming me?" he growled. "When you're the one who's so all-fired sexy and desirable and gorgeous—" He stopped in midsentence as the truth hit him. "A baby?" He couldn't take it in. "Jiminy Christmas, woman. We're gonna have a baby!"

Lifting her high in the air, he spun around and around, laughing like a madman. "I love you, Mrs. Murdock. This go-round I promise to do things right."

Kara's joyous face laughed back at him. "You're danged right you will. Now put me down before I get sick."

Ty eased her back to earth, then kissed her soundly. "Ah, Kara darlin', a year ago I was one miserable cowpoke. Who'da believed one little poker game could cause so much happiness?''

She gave a contented sigh and laid her head on his shoulder. "It's been quite a year, hasn't it?''

"Best year of my life.'' Every time he thought of all they'd accomplished together, he nearly burst with pride. With Kara's business sense and his contacts, they were quickly turning the Star M into a top provider of rodeo livestock. The ranch was growing, the fences fixed, the barns painted and repaired. His roots were firmly planted in east Texas soil. And he owed it all to this feisty woman.

Kara grinned up at him. "I'm so thankful you had the good sense to steal my ranch and force me to come home where I belonged.''

"Couldn't think of any other way to get my woman back.''

She'd willingly sold her interest in the Western-wear shop, sinking the profits into the Star M. She'd given him the strength and confidence to shuck his daddy's image and settle down for good. And now she was giving him another gift.

Taking her face in his hands, he said, "I hope we have a little girl with a sassy mouth and green eyes just like her mama.''

"Me, too,'' she answered, nipping his nose. "With you and Lane both around I'm outnumbered.''

Lane had been ecstatic to discover Ty was his natural father, and from that moment on he was Ty's sidekick and ally. The two identical grins were all it took for Kara to agree to anything they wanted.

Since the night they'd come home from Oklahoma City, a sleepy but exuberant Lane between them, Kara had done everything in her power to be the wife a man like Ty deserved. And she thanked her lucky stars she'd finally understood that love and truth are far more precious than pride and saving face.

Heart full to overflowing, Kara admitted, "A long time ago I wished for this."

"To stand in a dark cow lot with a crazy cowboy?" Ty's teeth gleamed white in the moonlight.

"No, silly." She whacked his chest. "To be this happy. To share our lives. To have another baby with you."

Ty's face softened. "I've thought of a name for her."

"Already?"

Kara followed Ty's gaze to the sequined northern sky. Her spirit soared as she guessed what he was about to say.

"Star," he murmured, coming closer, dark eyes glittering with love. "Star Murdock."

"Yes," she whispered against his warm mouth. "To remind us that sometimes wishes do come true."

Wrapped in love and moonlight, hearts beating as one, Kara and Ty sealed their love forever with a kiss. Around them, crickets pulsed a mating song. The scent of bluebonnets whispered on the spring air. And in the heavens above, a falling star added its own special blessing.

*   *   *   *   *

In her new miniseries,

Teresa Southwick

reveals what happens when a group of friends
return to their hometown: a place of lost loves,
budding dreams and enternal hope.

CRAZY FOR LOVIN' YOU
(SR #1529, July 2001)

THIS KISS
(SR #1541, September 2001)

IF YOU DON'T KNOW BY NOW
(SR #1560, December 2001)

and the final story
(SR #1572, February 2002)

Available at your favorite retail outlet.

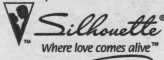

Where love comes alive™

Award-winning author
SHARON DE VITA
brings her special brand of romance to

Silhouette
SPECIAL EDITION™
and

SILHOUETTE ***Romance***™

in her new cross-line miniseries

SADDLE FALLS

This small Western town was rocked by scandal when the youngest son of the prominent Ryan family was kidnapped. Watch as clues about the mysterious disappearance are unveiled—and meet the sexy Ryan brothers...along with the women destined to lasso their hearts.

Don't miss:

WITH FAMILY IN MIND
February 2002, Silhouette Special Edition #1450

ANYTHING FOR HER FAMILY
March 2002, Silhouette Romance #1580

A FAMILY TO BE
April 2002, Silhouette Romance #1586

A FAMILY TO COME HOME TO
May 2002, Silhouette Special Edition #1468

Available at your favorite retail outlet.

Silhouette®
Where love comes alive™

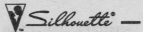

New from

a sperm bank mix-up sets a
powerful executive in search
of the woman who's...

DUE DATE:
Having the Boss's Baby

Don't miss any of these titles from
this exciting new miniseries:

WHEN THE LIGHTS WENT OUT...,
October 2001 by Judy Christenberry

A PREGNANT PROPOSAL,
November 2001 by Elizabeth Harbison

THE MAKEOVER TAKEOVER,
December 2001 by Sandra Paul

LAST CHANCE FOR BABY,
January 2002 by Julianna Morris

SHE'S HAVING MY BABY!,
February 2002 by Raye Morgan

Available at your favorite retail outlet.

Silhouette®
Where love comes alive™

Visit Silhouette at www.eHarlequin.com

SRHBB

If you enjoyed what you just read,
then we've got an offer you can't resist!

Take 2 bestselling love stories FREE!

Plus get a FREE surprise gift!

Clip this page and mail it to Silhouette Reader Service™

IN U.S.A.
3010 Walden Ave.
P.O. Box 1867
Buffalo, N.Y. 14240-1867

IN CANADA
P.O. Box 609
Fort Erie, Ontario
L2A 5X3

YES! Please send me 2 free Silhouette Romance® novels and my free surprise gift. After receiving them, if I don't wish to receive anymore, I can return the shipping statement marked cancel. If I don't cancel, I will receive 6 brand-new novels every month, before they're available in stores! In the U.S.A., bill me at the bargain price of $3.15 plus 25¢ shipping and handling per book and applicable sales tax, if any*. In Canada, bill me at the bargain price of $3.50 plus 25¢ shipping and handling per book and applicable taxes**. That's the complete price and a savings of at least 10% off the cover prices—what a great deal! I understand that accepting the 2 free books and gift places me under no obligation ever to buy any books. I can always return a shipment and cancel at any time. Even if I never buy another book from Silhouette, the 2 free books and gift are mine to keep forever.

215 SEN DFNQ
315 SEN DFNR

Name	(PLEASE PRINT)	
Address	Apt.#	
City	State/Prov.	Zip/Postal Code

* Terms and prices subject to change without notice. Sales tax applicable in N.Y.
** Canadian residents will be charged applicable provincial taxes and GST.
  All orders subject to approval. Offer limited to one per household and not valid to current Silhouette Romance® subscribers.
® are registered trademarks of Harlequin Enterprises Limited.

SROM01   ©1998 Harlequin Enterprises Limited